Give Me More Than Words

By

Katrina Avant

This book is a work of fiction and does not depict any person living or dead. The characters were created from the imagination of the author.

GIVE ME MORE THAN WORDS

Give Me More Than Words

Chapter 1

Justin

Justin Graham threw back his third scotch in an hour and dinner hadn't been served yet. He sat the crystal high ball down on the Egyptian cotton-covered table with a thud, grabbing the attention of his wife and daughter.

Casually, he eyed his wife's perfectly made-up face, letting his eyes drift to her tangerine-glossed lips; lips he had grown to hate, along with the body attached to them. Moving from his wife to their daughter, Justin noticed the child only vaguely glanced in his direction, before turning her attention back to her self-centered mother.

Sensing they were about to launch into another bitter argument, Anastasia called for Virginia to take the child to the nursery. Justin took this opportunity to signal the maid for another drink.

"Before you ask, no I haven't had nearly enough," Justin informed his frowning wife, cutting her off before she could speak.

Miss Allison brought him his requested drink, quickly leaving the room after doing so. She did not want to be a witness to the carnage that was sure to follow.

Anastasia brushed a stray hair from her peach-tinted cheek. She stared at her husband as he downed the expensive liquor in one swallow. He had been drinking a lot in the past few months, more so than usual. It started with an extra drink here and there, but as of late, it had been a few extras daily.

She glanced around the expensively decorated room, with the expensive artwork and custom, handmade furniture. With all of this, along with her money, and his thriving business, she felt Justin should be on cloud nine, and not in this depressive funk he had allowed himself to sink into. They made the perfect couple; the perfect family, along with their soon-to-be three-year-old daughter, Cara. At least she thought they had been perfect.

Anastasia Stanton-Graham refused to believe she'd made a mistake in choosing Justin for her husband. She thought with her money, and the doors it opened, it would be enough to keep him happily by her side. Who wouldn't want the life she gave him? He had everything a man could want and then some.

Sure, she had gotten pregnant purposefully, to ensure that he would be hers. But that was all par for the course. Besides, she recognized the hunger in Justin the moment she met him. He was ambitious, ambitious to the point he would do anything to ensure his plans would succeed. She had just helped those plans along and he should have been grateful.

But something was wrong and she didn't know what to make of it. It couldn't be Paige. That problem had gone away the moment she married her husband, Anderson Stone. So what was bothering her husband?

"I should never have married you," Justin was saying, bringing Anastasia out of her reflections.

"What did you say?" She asked him, not quite clear that she heard him correctly.

"I said, I should never have married you, Anastasia," he repeated while gazing at her through bloodshot eyes. Justin squeezed the back of his neck, trying to relieve the tension that had settled there.

"I should have stood up to you and not let you bully me into this marriage. I should have known this would not turn out well."

"How can you say that? You have your heart's desires," she retorted; her voice rising. "You have built the company of your dreams…no an empire! You have a wife…a daughter!" She sputtered in disbelief.

"Look around you Justin," she pressed, gesturing wildly with her arms. "You live in the lap of luxury…everything you could ever want at your fingertips!" Anastasia was livid. How could he sit there and say that?

"This…" Justin repeated her gesture flippantly, "was all acquired with *your* money Anastasia. Nothing in this room...hell nothing in my life reflects me. Even the success of my business is due to *your* money. I am a man bought and paid for, but I can't blame anyone but myself."

"You are such an ungrateful bastard! You would be nothing without me!"

"I would be happy without you," Justin spoke quietly, as he rose from his chair. He walked out of the dining room on unsteady legs, leaving Anastasia with her jaw hanging.

Justin Graham had made the biggest mistake of his life when he played a game he thought he controlled. He had purposely set out to seduce and deceive, to gain contracts for his company. In doing so, he had gotten the prize he coveted but lost the woman and the life that he loved. His greed had ensnared him in a trap set by a spoiled and selfish woman.

He felt he had no choice but to marry her, after she threatened to ruin him. Because of the pregnancy, and his need to build his business, he had agreed to this farce of a marriage. He foolishly believed he could sleep with her without consequences, all due to his reckless greed. But now, here he was living in Anastasia's mansion, surrounded by wealth he had nothing to do with. He was an acquired man and he was in hell.

Swaying his way into his room, Justin picked up the in-house phone to call Miss Allison for another drink. It seemed that was all he did once he stepped over the threshold of Anastasia's home. He tried staying away as much as possible. He kept his company's headquarters in his home state, where he spent most of his time. He only flew "home" on the weekends, at his wife's demand.

Justin sighed. He had come to a decision. He had to leave Anastasia. He couldn't spend another night under the same roof with her. Although he had moved out of their shared bedroom a year ago, he was still under her thumb.

Glancing around the lavishly decorated room, he thought about their daughter, Cara. Justin slowly shook his head. Anastasia had insisted on giving the girl a name that meant love as if doing so would magically bring the emotion into their lives. There was anything but love in their household.

Shaking his head again, he picked up a photo of his wife and daughter from the nightstand. Concentrating only on his daughter, Justin cringed. Cara was an exact replica of her mother—spoiled and selfish. He placed the crystal-framed portrait back in the spot where her mother had placed it; seemingly to remind him of his place in their lives, which was on the outskirts, where Anastacia had firmly positioned him. She hadn't even bothered to acquire a photo with the three of them.

Surrendering, Justin sighed again. Cara wouldn't miss him. The girl took cues from her mother; ignoring him, unless she wanted something from him. This was rare since her mother gave her everything. Giving the room a final distasteful sweep, Justin pulled his bags from the closet to pack his things.

#

Anastasia Stanton-Graham sat staring blankly at the chair her husband had vacated. She couldn't believe Justin didn't want her. She gave him everything: money, power, prestige. What more could he have asked for?

Closing her eyes, she had to admit. Although their union should have been happy, it was not. She thought once they were married, they would grow to love each other. However, after three years, they had not. She was greatly fond of Justin, but she didn't love him. She now knew he could never love her.

Their union had started rocky, even after she helped him handle his attachment to Page Bennett. After she had flown down to Aruba to collect him, Anastasia had made things clear to him. Justin had gone there to make trouble for his former girlfriend and her fiancé. In doing so, he had gotten himself arrested. Anastasia had been furious. She made sure he understood the consequences if he failed to drop his obsession with Paige. Finally, Paige was married and out of their lives. So why wasn't Justin content with her and what she gave him?

"Mrs. Stanton-Graham?" Virginia, Cara's nanny called to her. Anastasia hadn't heard the woman enter the room.

"Yes Virginia, what is it?" She was annoyed with the intrusion. She wanted to know how to regain control of her husband, not to be interrupted by the help.

"Ma'am, Cara is asking for you. She wants you to read her a bedtime story," Virginia hesitantly informed her employer.

Virginia recognized the expression on Anastasia's face and wished to avoid any kind of confrontation. Especially now, after she saw Justin leaving with his belongings. She wondered what would happen once she learned of his departure. Anastasia was known for her rages when she didn't get her way.

"Not tonight Virginia," Anastasia told her, as she rose from her chair. "I must talk to my husband. Explain to Cara that I will see her first thing in the morning."

"Ma'am, Mr. Graham left thirty minutes ago." Virginia hesitantly informed her of this with increasing dread. She was sure this self-serving woman would take it out on her.

Anastasia sighed. "Did he say when he would return?" She asked, plopping back into her chair.

"Umm…Ma'am…I don't think he's coming back," Virginia informed her, dreading her reaction even more.

"What do you mean you don't think he's coming back?" Eyes narrowed, Anastasia rose from her chair again, this time heading for Justin's suite of rooms.

Virginia started after her. "Mrs., he had most of his belongings with him," she quickly added. This stopped Anastasia in her tracks.

Virginia pressed forward. "The chauffeur took him to the airport…and I overheard Mr. Graham instructing Miss Allison to pack up what was left. He told her he would send for those things later."

Virginia watched her employer turn and race up the stairs. Heaving a sigh of relief, she went to care for her charge. Anastasia had bigger concerns than her.

#

Justin boarded the private jet for the last time. He knew once Anastasia found he had left her, she would take everything from him, so he would enjoy this last flight in luxury. Settling himself in the comfortably soft leather seat, he breathed a long-deserved sigh of relief. It was finally over. He had gotten away from his tyrant of a wife.

☐

Chapter 2

Dani

"Wow, can you believe Andee and Tor are married?" Paige Stone asked her husband as they relaxed on the sofa. They were enjoying the quiet of the evening.

"Yeah, that was some surprise," Anderson responded.

"But the bigger question is, what's going on with Dani and Devin? I asked Devin when they would be jumping the broom and the question seemed to make him uneasy. What's up with that?" Anderson asked his wife.

She shrugged. "Dani said they agreed they didn't need to get married. Although, I suspect there is more to it. I wonder if Devin has something to do with her take on marriage." Paige pondered more to herself than actually speaking to her husband.

Anderson shook his head in disagreement. "I don't think so. Devin clearly wants to be married. Dani is the one that's not interested."

Deep in thought, Paige made a mental note to get to the bottom of this perplexing situation.

#

Devin watched Dani nervously move around the room. She had been uneasy all afternoon, more so after they returned to his home from the cookout at the Stones. She was chattering away about the surprise of the day, their friends', unexpected elopement. He knew why she had become uncomfortable—the subject of marriage. Once again, the topic had made an appearance in their lives. He was more than ready to marry the love of his life, but she wasn't. What's more, she would not give him a straight answer as to why she wouldn't marry him. Whenever the subject arose, she would quickly change it.

When he first laid eyes on Dani Sinclair, Devin pictured her as his wife, not a woman he would be in a perpetual long-standing relationship with. He remembered the first time she came to his home. He was in awe. He never believed in love at first sight, until he met Dani.

Devin had commissioned her to decorate his home; at least that was the ruse he used to get her there. He first noticed her at a charity event they both had attended. After inquiring about her, he learned she was an interior designer, prompting him to commission her to work for him, so he would have an excuse to meet her.

When she came to his home the second time, to discuss color schemes, he had seduced her, and she had willingly followed his lead. He knew she felt the same way he did from that moment on. He just didn't know what had changed since then.

"I never would have thought Andee would have eloped," she was saying. "I knew she and Tor were headed towards marriage, but not this soon."

"Dani, why won't you marry me?" Devin asked her softly, interrupting her rambling. He felt he deserved an answer right then and there.

Dani stopped rearranging the books on a nearby table and turned to answer him. She knew eventually Devin would want an answer, and she had thought of what she would say. But at the moment, she was at a loss for words. She felt she couldn't explain to him why she couldn't marry him, without revealing her secret. She knew she would have to tell him everything if she entered into an agreement, as serious as marriage. Dani vowed she would never tell another living soul of the choices she made; choices which changed her life forever.

"Devin, I can't marry you," she told him matter-of-factly. She knew he wanted an explanation, but she couldn't give him one.

"What do you mean you can't marry me? Why not?" Devin was overcome with her answer of can't.

Chapter 3

Jean

Alfra-Jean Wilson, Jean, as she was known to most people, stared at her reflection in the full-length mirror. She turned slowly from front to back. Gradually, a smile spread across her slim face. She liked what she saw. Jean never thought she could look this good. She couldn't believe that for years, she had wasted her time going to the gym chasing after men, who didn't want her when she could have been improving herself. She shook her head. All that valuable time was wasted.

Jean was five foot one but told people she was five-three as if a couple of inches would make a lot of difference. For most of her life she had been overweight, and to add to this unhealthy trait, she had horrendously worn unflattering hairstyles that created a peculiar appearance that everyone saw but her. Inspecting her lightly enhanced face, she shamefully remembered the mask of cosmetics she used to wear, along with clothes that were too tight and inappropriate for her heavy frame.

She closed her eyes, in further embarrassment, when she recalled the asinine behavior she used to ooze, all because she was unhappy with herself. Jean had taken most of her self-loathing out on Paige, her boyfriend's sister because she was jealous of how she looked. Paige was beautiful, and Jean could never see herself as lovely as she saw her self-appointed rival. But now, looking in the mirror at her transformation, she smiled enthusiastically.

She had finally lost the weight that had plagued most of her life. She had ditched the clown make-up and sported clothes she looked fabulous in. This was all due to Evan Bennett. He brought out in her what she never before recognized in herself.

Although Evan was attracted to her, as she had been when he first met her, his attention had motivated her to make changes in her life. She started going to the gym to work out and not to flirt with men. This move alone drew curious stares from the regulars who knew her and loathed her.

Norma, her hair stylist, also noticed the change. She didn't bully her way into the salon, demanding to look like a replica of some hideous atrocity she had dug out of her oversized purse. She now wore her own full, shoulder-length hair, which Norma kept expertly colored and styled.

Slowly, people began to warm up to the new Jean. They began to like the woman she had become. It was a major change from the vile person who spread gossip and ill will wherever she went. No one knew that better than Evan's sister. However, Jean had made peace with her and turned her life around. She was just grateful Paige and her friends had forgiven her for her transgressions.

Checking her platinum vintage watch, Jean grinned happily. Evan would be there soon. He was in town just to see her and she was ecstatic. Since meeting, at his sister's wedding, he visited her regularly. Although he saw his sister from time to time, his trips were mainly to spend time with her. Jean never thought she could be with a man, as intelligent and handsome as Evan Bennett.

Though Jean had been married before, her husband had been average at best. And it hadn't helped that he only married her for her money. It was a good thing she had an air-tight prenup.

The doorbell chimed. Jean checked her watch again. "Right on time." She smiled, as she picked up her purse and keys before heading for the door.

While he waited for Jean to answer her door, Evan had a smile of his own.

Evan Bennett was the CEO of a major aerospace corporation. He started as one of the company's engineers and had worked his way through the ranks to become top man. Although he loved his job, he was grateful for today's technology, which didn't require him to be tethered to a desk to do it. This allowed him to entertain Jean as much as he liked, and he liked it a lot. He was very fond of the 'little woman', as he affectionately called her. Compared to his height, of six feet three, she was indeed his little woman.

His smile widened when he thought of his friends teasing him about the 'little woman'. Jean was not his usual type. He was known to date women who were model height with the superficial beauty and size to match. But what his friends failed to see, those women were a dime a dozen and usually just as shallow. Evan had grown tired of the narcissistic crowd. He craved a woman who wasn't self-absorbed, a woman who was real—a woman of substance. He found that in Jean.

However, when he met her, he understood she and his sister had some conflict, but they soon worked through it. Also at the time, Jean wore a little too much make-up and her clothes were a bit tight, but Evan was able to see passed the overly made-up face and clothes Jean frequently wore. Those things were just surface and could be worked with.

At the time, he believed she didn't see herself as an attractive woman. He knew, because of her weight, she overcompensated for what she felt she lacked, as a woman. In his opinion, she couldn't have been more wrong. She was beautiful. She just needed to see and believe it for herself.

"Evan." Jean breathlessly spoke his name the moment she pulled open the door. He immediately took her into his arms, lifting her off her feet to kiss her.

"Mmm," he moaned, releasing her. "You sure you want to go out tonight?"

He had been trying to get her into bed for the past few visits, but she wasn't ready. Even though she had lost weight and looked fabulous, Jean was still self-conscious about her body. He was just glad she hadn't lost too much weight. He loved her curvy size eight. He had grown tired of the wafer-thin women.

"I'll tell you what," Jean was saying. "We will go out as planned and then come back here to continue our date. And yes you may stay the night," she told him before he could ask. In the past, he would have ended the date back at his hotel alone.

Jean was finally ready to take that next step. She knew she had to get over her phobia about her body. It wasn't the same as it had been when she first met him, but it still took some time for her to get used to the new Jean. She had carried that size eighteen body around for most of her life, so it took a while to accept that it was gone and never to return. She was determined to make sure of that.

Smiling happily, Evan pressed some numbers on the keypad to lock her door. Taking her hand, he led her to his car.

Chapter 4

Jayden

After his flight home, Jayden maneuvered his way through the crowded terminal. Even though the airport was swarming with travelers, he hadn't noticed. His mind was still reeling from the revelation of Andee's marriage.

He had flown in to attend his cousin's engagement party. With a little help from Taylor's insistence, he had finally gotten up the nerve to go. He knew Andee would be there with Tor, but he felt the need to see her again. He wanted to personally apologize for his behavior, which led to their break-up.

They hadn't spoken since he stormed out of her house, over his self-righteous judgment of her. Jayden felt, not only did he owe her an apology, but needed to ask for her forgiveness. Also, he wanted to see if they had a chance to give their relationship another try. However, all was lost the moment he heard Tor tell the guys he and Andee were married.

Jayden had just let himself into his brother's backyard when he heard the squeals from the women in the kitchen. He wondered what the commotion was all about. That was before he heard Tor tell the group in the yard the big news. He had backed out of there before anyone noticed him. He couldn't breathe. He felt as if someone had punched him in the gut.

Andee married. Making his way back to his rental, he sat stunned. Andee married. He couldn't blame anyone but himself. Closing his eyes, he rested his head against the headrest, struggling hard to control his emotions. Finally getting himself under control, he started the car and drove back to the airport.

Pulling himself from the past, he finally became aware that he was navigating through a sea of people. He turned to look around, just before he heard a yelp. He turned back just in time to prevent the woman he bumped into, from falling to the floor. He couldn't say as much for her bags, as they skidded across the terminal.

\#

Hannah Pierce was tired, and the last thing she needed was a crowded airport. She had been running around for days, trying to get everything into place before her move. It seemed each time she completed one task, another one appeared on her list of things to do. She had finally gotten her house sold, which had been her final task, moments before boarding the plane to her new life.

Hannah had enough of her hometown. She had been feeling weary of the place for a while. It took the failure of her last relationship, to push her along. The first thing she did was put her home up for sale. She prayed that, in this economy, she would be able to sell it quickly. God must have heard her prayers because the house was sold within three months of the listing.

She thanked her lucky stars that she didn't need to find a job in her new city. Being a freelance writer gave her the freedom to perform her work from any place on earth, so long as she had her laptop and a reliable internet connection. Income would not be a problem.

The only difficulty at the moment was navigating through the overly populated airport, and hopefully to a waiting taxi outside. She had just grabbed her last piece of luggage and had turned to place it on the cart when she was bumped—hard.

"Hey, will you watch where you're going…dammit!" Hannah's bags tumbled all across the floor as she fell into the cart. She was just about to follow them when a hand reached out to steady her, preventing her from landing on top of the overturned luggage cart.

"I'm sorry Miss. I should have been paying more attention," Jayden apologized, as he righted the angry woman.

"Yes you should have," Hannah hissed. She snatched her arm from his grasp. Letting out a huge sigh of frustration, she proceeded to retrieve her scattered bags.

"May I at least help you?" He asked, bending to gather a bag that someone nearly tripped over.

"No, I think you have done quite enough, thank you." Hannah placed the last bag on the cart before she looked up at the man who had caused all of the commotion.

Humph, another jerk who probably thought he was God's gift to women, she thought. She gave him the once over; tall, gorgeous, and arrogant. She knew the type and she'd had her fill. Hannah felt he may have knocked her over on purpose, just to have a quick pick-up line.

Not tonight, she thought. She was too tired and weary from her flight to even entertain the thought of getting to know him. Besides, at the moment, her new life didn't include men. She'd had her fill of relationships as well.

After dismissing him with a roll of her eyes, Hannah shouldered her purse and strolled off with her luggage, leaving Jayden staring after her.

He watched the irate woman rapidly push the cart through the crowd of people. Jaden studied her. She was tall and shapely, with long reddish brown hair. The jeans she wore hugged her in all the right places, along with the tie-dyed tee shirt she wore.

He only got a chance to look at her face for a moment, but he remembered it clearly. Her skin was a smooth golden brown, small perky nose, with clear dark eyes that seemed to sparkle, even in the terminal's poor lighting. Although she had been frowning, he imagined she had a great smile just the same.

Jayden shook himself out of his daydream, as he accepted he would probably never see her again. Just as well, he wasn't over Andee. Pulling his own bag more securely onto his shoulder, he followed the mystery woman's path towards the parking garage.

☐

Chapter 5

Nicolas

Jean loved spending time with Evan. When he
wasn't visiting with her, she was flying to San Francisco to
spend time with him.

They dined at a restaurant where the maître d knew
them by name. Jean loved the food there, even though she
tried to count the calories in each entrée. Evan had made it
clear that he didn't mind that she had a little meat on her
bones. Nevertheless, he understood she wanted to maintain
her weight and supported her efforts.

The couple enjoyed a wonderful meal, along with a
night of great conversation, after which they arrived back at
Jean's home. Evan was excited. He was finally going to
show her how much he cared for her. He couldn't wait to
undress her. They were strolling up the expertly laid
cobblestone walk, with Jean laughing at Evan's off-key
singing, when a figure stepped out of the shadows, startling
them both.

"Jean," the man said as he came into view under the Spanish-styled lighting. Evan stepped forward to protect her.

"Who the hell are you and what are you doing here?" Evan asked the stranger. He was ready to do battle if need be.

"Jean," the man spoke again, ignoring Evan. Evan made a move towards him, only to be stopped by Jean.

"Evan wait! He's my ex-husband," she told him, grabbing his arm.

"What do you want Nicolas?" She asked of her former husband. She hadn't seen the man, since their divorce three years ago.

"I would like to talk to you a moment…please," Nicolas added, all the while eyeing Evan's clenched jaw.

"And before you say there is nothing to talk about, please give me a chance and hear me out." He spoke this last sentence, more to Evan than he did to Jean. Nicolas could see that he was more than ready to get rid of him.

"You have exactly five minutes, Nicolas," she told him. Jean turned to Evan, who leaned down to kiss her on her upturned lips.

"It's okay. Why don't I give you two sometime…that is unless you want me to stay?" He added, still eyeing Nicolas.

Jean sighed. "No, it's okay. How about I see you in the morning for breakfast?" She asked apologetically. She knew how much this evening meant to him, to both of them, but she needed to see what her ex could possibly want considering they no longer had any reason to interconnect.

Kissing her again, Evan turned and eyed Nicolas one last time before leaving.

Jean opened her door to let them inside. Nicolas followed her into the sunken room, looking around as he did so. He noticed she had made quite a few changes since he was there last. Gone was the old antique furniture that he loathed. She had replaced it with Spanish and Southwestern style furnishings and accents, which gave the house life.

And thinking of changes, he brought his eyes back to her body. She was stunning. The pale yellow dress she wore was molded to her shapely frame. It hugged her breasts and hips as if it were made just for them. The four-inch gold spiked heels, accentuated her toned legs.

She was so unlike the overweight, vicious woman whom he had left three years ago. He almost hadn't recognized her, when he first spotted her a few weeks earlier in the mall. She was dressed to impress. Her hair was beautifully styled; hair he never saw when they were married. She always wore those awful extensions.

He wanted her. Sure, he was only there for money, but now that she had transformed into this beauty, he wanted some of her as well.

"What do you want Nicolas?" Jean asked him again, as she settled herself on the sofa.

She never expected to see this man again. When they divorced, she had paid him a hefty sum, but it was worth it to get rid of him. And it was certainly worth it, to keep him from contesting the pre-nup, which would have dragged the agony on for years. The only reason she could think that he had shown up again, would be to try to get more money out of her. She had heard through the grapevine that he was broke. Not surprising, since he never liked to work.

"I realized the mistake I made in letting you go, Jean. I miss you. I love you. I didn't know how much, until after we divorced. I know we parted ways…well with some difficulty, but I would love to try again. What do you say? I know you still love me."

Jean stared at her former husband as if he had lost his mind. Is this what she let Evan leave for? Surely this is a joke, she thought. This man had cheated their entire marriage until he finally left her for some cheap stripper he had met at the local booty bar, as she liked to call the club he consistently visited.

Staring at him, Jean grew angrier with each breath. She wondered if it was too late to call Evan back—after she put this fool out.

"Nicolas dear," she said sweetly. "If you don't get the HELL OUT OF MY HOUSE...," she started.

Before she could finish her sentence, Evan strolled swiftly into the room, grabbing a startled Nicolas by the back of his collar.

"I believe the lady asked you to leave," Evan told him through clenched teeth, as he roughly showed him to the door.

Jean heard her door open, and then close with a resounding bang. She waited for Evan to return.

"Evan...how?...what...," she stammered. He had caught her by surprise as well.

"You couldn't possibly think I would leave you alone with that clown, did you?" He pulled her to him, with the beginnings of a smile spreading across her face.

"I'm glad you didn't," she told him. Grateful, she pulled his face to hers to thank him.

This time Evan did lift her off her feet. He carried her to the nearest wall, where he pressed her back against. Holding her there effortlessly, he pulled the straps of her dress from her shoulders, exposing her size C, bra-encased breasts. He kissed the tops of each one, as he pushed the hem of her dress up to her waist, exposing her gold lace panties. Jean found herself moaning with anticipation.

With her still pressed against the wall and him pressed against her, Evan unzipped his fly. Pulling the crotch of her panties to one side, he entered her. They both cried out from the instant contact. Jean wrapped her legs around him as he thrust inside of her, pushing her up the wall as he did so, bringing her more pleasure than she thought she could handle. Evan continued to thrust until his legs began to weaken, forcing him to stop to take a moment to recover.

With Jean still firmly wrapped around him, Evan carried her upstairs to her bedroom, where he placed her across the king-sized wrought iron sleigh bed. Not wanting to break contact, but needing to feel her bare skin against his, Evan withdrew from her protesting body.

He made quick work of undressing them both, before climbing onto the bed to enter her again. He rode her feverishly, bringing them both uncontained pleasure. Jean called his name repeatedly, nearly losing her breath with each syllable.

Unable to hold back any longer, Evan drove faster, deeper, until finally bringing an end to their ride. Breathing heavily, he gathered Jean into his arms, as he rolled off of her, completely satisfied. Kissing her forehead, Evan tightened his grip on her as they drifted to sleep.

#

Nicolas Hampton paced the length of his small living room. He was worried. He couldn't believe he'd been thrown out of his ex-wife's house. If he didn't come up with the money to pay his bookie soon, he was a dead man.

While he paced, he thought about Jean. When they were married, she looked okay in the face, but her body was not to be coveted. He had her pegged for no self-esteem the moment he met her. It had been easy to wine and dine her into marriage. She had believed he was her only chance.

But now, with her transformation from ugly duck to beautiful woman, she was dripping with self-esteem and confidence. Making it almost impossible to persuade her to take him back. And it didn't help that she had a man in her life; a real man.

This dude Evan hadn't figured into his plan to sweet-talk Jean into taking him back. When he first met Jean, no one would have her. But now, things have changed. Not only did she have a man, he could tell Evan was money, which put him on an even playing field with Jean. She had no reason to take him back. Why would she?

Alfra-Jean Wilson was old money. Back before she was born, her father had played the stock markets like a well-tuned instrument, netting him millions, if not billions of dollars. No one was quite sure of his actual worth. All anyone knew was his only daughter would never have to work a day in her life. Unfortunately for Nicolas, he hadn't found out her true worth, until after the divorce. He shook his head at that one. Had he known, he would have tolerated her come what may.

"Dammit, dammit, DAMMIT!" Nicolas kicked a pillow he had thrown to the floor earlier out of frustration. His hands shook as he thought about the thugs who would beat him senseless if he didn't come up with the seventy-five grand he owed their boss.

Nicolas Hampton made a tidy sum off of his divorce from Jean. He had grinned all the way to the bank. Even though he had been the one to cheat, he had made out like a bandit, all because Alfra-Jean wanted to hide her failure as a wife. He never really liked her. She had only been his meal ticket at the time. She had been one of many through the years.

Nicolas made his living traveling around the country, making wealthy women happy, since he was a teen. His usual clientele were rich, bored housewives, who needed a pick me up from time to time, when their rich husbands ignored them for their own playthings.

Jean was different. She didn't have a husband, which made it easy for him to play to her insecurities and marry her. Before the ink was dry on their marriage license, he was spending her money in every way he could. He bought the finest of clothes, cars—and women.

Although he wouldn't admit it, Nicolas didn't have much going for himself other than his ability to charm and satisfy lonely women. Dropping out of school after the eleventh grade, he had no formal education. His appearance at best was average, along with his height. His chocolate brown skin was accentuated by dark brows and a thin mustache. He was a thin spindly man, whose saving grace was his naturally curly hair, which seemed to draw quite a few women.

Now he was broke and in desperate need of some quick cash. He swallowed hard at this thought. It was the need for quick cash that had gotten him into this mess. He should have stayed away from the strip clubs, especially his favorite, *Caitee Cat's Lair*, where he met sweet Lucinda.

Lucinda had been his undoing. He was drawn back night after night until he was completely under her spell. After a while, they started seeing each other outside of the club, which was the first mistake he made. The second was falling for Lucinda—hard. She did things to him that he usually reserved for his marks. Nicolas soon found himself caught up in his own game. He found himself spending money, big money on whatever Lucinda wanted. That was until he was down to a few thousand dollars.

To try to build on the money he had left, to continue to keep Lucinda happy, he started betting with a bookie. At first, things were fine. He was betting and winning back-to-back. But his greed got the best of him and he let it all ride on a supposed sure thing, losing it all and then some. This is what led to his current predicament. Fye Freddy was looking to get his money and he didn't have it.

Nicolas continued to pace the floor, trying to come up with another plan. He had turned to make another sweep of the room when someone knocked on his door. He froze. Had Freddy's goons found him? The knock came again, but this time with a female voice.

"Nicolas? Nicolas honey open the door…it's me!" It was Lucinda.

Nicolas almost wept with relief. Hurrying to the door, he checked the peephole to make sure she was alone. Satisfied that she was, he opened the door just enough for her to squeeze through.

"Nicolas, what's wrong honey? I've been calling you for hours. Why didn't you answer your phone?"

Lucinda was your typical stripper. She sported a long, blonde, lace-front wig, spandex, and man-made boobs with an IQ to match. Today she donned a fire engine red halter-topped dress that barely covered the tops of her thighs.

"I couldn't get the money," he told her nervously. "I couldn't get the damn money!" He repeated, shaking even more.

"Well, what happened?" Lucinda asked, wide-eyed. "You said you had a foolproof plan baby," she whined.

"I know, I know what I said." Nicholas started his pacing again. "I didn't figure on the bitch having a man in her life. I thought I could sweet talk my way back and into her bank account… but now…," he trailed off, knowing it would be impossible for him to get close to Jean, now with Mr. Hero hanging around.

"So what we gonna do now baby?" Lucinda pouted. She saw all of those dollars slipping away.

He was so sure his plan would work that he would not only get enough money to pay off Fye Freddy but some extra for them to leave town and start fresh; maybe Vegas. Lucinda always talked about seeing Vegas. She had aspirations of being a showgirl.

"I don't know baby, I don't know," he told her, after an anxious sigh.

#

Fye Freddy watched while someone let Lucinda into Hampton's apartment. And from the way the door was opened to allow her entrance, he knew it had to be Nicolas himself. So the little weasel didn't have his money. Freddy smirked at the little man's cowardice. He would get his money, oh yes he would, or he would enjoy every painful moment of taking it out of Nicolas's hide. Satisfied with his plan, Fye Freddy pulled away from the curb, merging his silver Range Rover into traffic.

Chapter 6

Jayden

Jayden dragged himself out of the shower and crawled into his bed. He had just gotten home from working one of the worst fires the city had ever seen. A ten-story apartment building with several people trapped inside.

His department had gotten there first and was in the process of fighting the blaze when two children appeared at a sixth-floor window. His Lieutenant had given him the task of rescuing them from the outside, while his fellow firefighters fought the blaze from within. This would have been simple had one of the children not panicked and jumped from the window, before the basket Jayden was in, had reached them. Jayden was grateful he was able to catch the child before he plunged to his death.

After rescuing the falling child, the platform operator finally maneuvered him into position to reach the boy's sister. The children's mother had run down the block to the corner store when the fire broke out. Most of the other residents had evacuated the building, except for the two children and an elderly couple who were afraid to leave their apartment. Jayden brought the children safely down to the street where their anxious mother was waiting. The elderly couple had been rescued by his coworkers working inside the building. He was glad the day had a happy ending.

Jayden was grateful that his twenty-four-hour shift was up and he didn't have to return to the firehouse for a couple of days. He needed to sleep in his bed. He loved his job, but it was hard being among the crew, pretending everything was ok when he was still reeling from Andee's marriage. Just as he drifted to sleep, his phone rang. He couldn't believe it. He was on the verge of getting the best sleep he'd had in days.

Cursing softly he answered the phone. "Hello, and this better be good," he muttered tightly. There was a moment's pause before the caller responded.

"Hello, yes…Mr. Stone?" The female voice asked.

"Yes, this is Jayden Stone, what do you want?" He was hoping for this lady's sake, she was not a telemarketer, or else she was about to hear some very harsh words.

"Mr. Stone, my name is Hannah Pierce and I write for a local magazine. We learned of your heroic efforts in saving the two children from the fire earlier this morning. I would like to interview you for an article I'm writing. Would that be possible?" She asked.

Jayden paused. In all the years he had been on his job, he had never been interviewed and he wasn't sure he wanted to start. He was about to tell the caller he wasn't interested when she spoke again.

"Mr. Stone, I won't take up much of your time, as I know how valuable time is, with the work that you do, but I am sure my readers would like to get some insight into what it must be like to do your job." Hannah hoped this would clinch it for her. She could sense he was about to say no.

Sighing, Jayden responded. "When and where?"

"How about tomorrow…say noon, at BJ's coffee shop on Vance. Do you know it?" Hannah happily replied.

"Yeah, I know where it is and I will meet you there…Ms. Pierce is it?"

"Yes, and thank you, Mr. Stone. I will see you tomorrow." With that, she was gone.

Placing the phone on its charger, Jayden lay back into his pillow, hoping he wouldn't regret his decision.

Chapter 7

Dani

Jayden wasn't the only one unable to sleep.

Dani Sinclair sat in her office trying to stop the flow of tears. She came in early because she couldn't sleep. Tired of tossing and turning, she decided to get up and come in to get some work done.

She had been having sleepless nights after telling Devin she could not marry him, and walking out without giving him an explanation. She had broken things off with him. The only thing she could do under the circumstances. She couldn't stay, knowing they had no future.

She had been happy with their relationship until he expressed the fact he wanted to marry her. She could have handled that had he not added the second request—for her to be the mother of his children. That was the deal breaker. If he had wanted anything but that.

Dani loved children, but because of her reckless actions, she could not bring any into the world herself. Outside of her brother, no one knew what happened when she was in college, not even her best friends, Paige and Andee. And she preferred to keep it that way.

Tears continued to stream down her face, because of her choice to let him go. She couldn't marry Devin under those circumstances. She loved him and hated herself for the hurt she had placed in his life. She should have known better than to let him get close to her. He deserved more than she could give him.

Wiping away the fallen tears, Dani quickly scribbled a note to Andee and Paige. Grabbing her purse, she had made a decision. She needed some time alone to figure things out. One thing she knew for certain, her relationship with Devin was over.

#

Devin stared at the photo of him and Dani. He shook his head in disbelief. He wanted to know why she left him. She may have thought things were over between them, but he knew better. There was no way he was going to allow her to walk away that easily.

Chapter 8

Jean

Evan pulled Jean up from the floor. They had spent the early morning jogging and had gotten back to her place to finish their workout. They continued their exercises for about an hour, running through Jean's routine, when he suggested some sit-ups to finish up. Jean had lain on her back, knees up and hands behind her head, while Evan anchored her feet.

She had done about ten, before Evan's hands wandered from her feet, along her calves, until they made their way up to her thighs. She stopped and peered at him from her place on the floor. His eye color had changed. Something she noticed whenever he was aroused. They had spent the better part of the night before making love. This man was insatiable and she didn't mind one bit.

Waiting to see what he would do next, Jean watched while he pulled his black tank top over his head. He stood to scramble out of his shoes, gym shorts, and underwear.

With this done, Evan resumed his kneeling position. He took his time, as he untied and pulled Jean's sneakers from her feet, with her watching his every move. Throwing the shoes to the side, he gripped the waistband of her gray running shorts, pulling them, along with her panties, from her body. Jean quivered with anticipation.

Without speaking a word, Evan continued his assault on her senses. He slid his palms under her sports bra, cupping her breasts, massaging them slowly and methodically. Finally lifting the bra up and over, exposing her full breasts, he drew it over her head.

Tossing this too aside, he parted her knees and settled himself between her thighs, drawing her legs up and over his shoulders. Taking one of her breasts into his hand, he drew its nipple into his mouth, teasing it with his tongue and teeth, drawing moans and more shivers from Jean. Grasping its twin, Evan moved to the other breast, repeating the motions with his mouth.

While Evan teased and caressed her breasts, Jean moved her hands south, finding the treasure she sought.

Gently she cupped his boys with one hand, as she slid the other the length of his long thick shaft. This brought moans from him, as she applied just enough pressure to drive him out of his mind.

Not able to wait any longer, Evan grabbed both of her wrists, pinning them above her head. Lowering his lips to hers, he thrust his tongue into her mouth, as he pushed inside of her. Releasing her wrists, he palmed her hips, lifting them, as he rotated his own to drive deeper inside of her. This brought shouts of satisfaction from them both.

Evan moved inside of Jean until they both neared their peak. Sensing she was about to tumble over the edge, Evan drove even faster, with Jean matching him thrust for thrust, pushing them both over. Catching his breath, he got up reaching for Jean's hand. Pulling her to her feet, he lifted the little woman, to carry her to the shower.

Had Jean looked over Evan's shoulder, she would have caught the shadow of someone leaving the window outside.

#

Nicolas got out of his car with a cigarette dangling from his lips. A nervous habit he had picked up after losing his money to Fye Freddy. Cautiously, he looked around to see if any of Freddy's goons were waiting for him, as he made his way to his apartment.

After Lucinda left, he drove around most of the night not knowing what to do next. As the sun rose, he decided to drive out to his ex-wife's again. He had hoped Mr. Hero was gone. He had to take one last shot at getting Jean back, but no such luck. Not only was her lover there, he had caught them screwing on the matted floor of her exercise room. This had upset him. There was no way he could get her back, after viewing that scene.

"Maybe I should just find another broad to tap into," he muttered to himself.

The problem with that plan, he didn't think he would have the time to break in a new mark. Besides, Lucinda hungrily agreed with him trying to fleece his ex, she would be none too happy if she learned he was trying to hook up with a new woman.

Nicolas was walking swiftly to his apartment, when he rounded a corner and caught a fist to the gut, knocking the half-smoked cigarette from his mouth. One of Freddy's thugs had punched him.

"Oof." Nicolas crumbled to his knees, only to have the man give him a fist to the face, knocking him backward. Rolling around on the ground in agony, he looked up as Fye Freddy came into view.

"Nicolas, Nicolas my man. Looks like you fell down," Freddy commented, shaking his head in feigned pity. "I take it you don't have my money, Nicolas. What shall we do about that?" Fye Freddy walked around Nicolas, as he lay writhing on the ground. Bending near him, Freddy patted him on the cheek.

"I'll tell you what. Since I like you, and I do like you Nicolas, maybe we can come to some arrangement. See, after you left your place last night, my boys had a look around. They found something interesting. Do you know what that was Nicolas?" Freddy asked him. Nicolas coughed and shook his head. "They found your way out of this mess."

"Stand him up," Freddy gruffly told one of his men. The man roughly picked Nicolas up from the ground. "How about you and I go into your place to discuss my proposition," Freddy told him, as the two men dragged him inside.

☐

Chapter 9

Evan

Evan came fully awake from a sound he was sure was a dream. He had fallen asleep in Jean's bed, waiting for her to return with their dinner.

"Evan!" came Jean's high-pitched scream.

Bounding from the bed, he quickly realized this was no dream. Sprinting down the hallway and the stairs, he followed Jean's voice, which sounded on the edge of hysteria. It was when he rounded the corner into the kitchen, that he skidded to a stop.

Visibly shaking, Jean's eyes pointed to her fright. Coiled in the middle of the kitchen floor was a diamondback rattlesnake trained on her.

Evan's heart raced into overdrive as he assessed the situation. "Baby don't move," he told a frightened Jean. Trying to think how he would get her out unharmed, he quickly had an idea.

"Do you have a mop or…or a broom nearby?" he asked.

"Ye…yes, there is a dust mop in the closet behind you," she told him. Moving quietly he found the mop.

"Is there a butcher's knife…any kind of big knife near you?" He had a plan. He just hoped she wouldn't be too frightened to help him.

Jean indicated there was one in the draw to her left. He instructed her to grab the knife as soon as he covered the snake's head with the mop. Still trained on Jean, it hadn't noticed Evan was in the room. Jean looked as if she would faint at the thought of having to move from her cemented spot, but she knew she had to try.

"Okay, when I say now, pass me the knife and grab the mop handle. Make sure you keep it pressed firmly down on its head. Do you think that you can do that?" He hoped for both of their sakes she would not panic. Jean nodded.

Here goes nothing Evan thought. He eased up behind the snake. When he got close enough, he brought the rectangular mop down on its head, hard; pinning it to the floor.

"Now!" He yelled. Quickly opening the draw, Jean handed him the knife as she grabbed the mop handle with both hands, forcing it down with all her might.

As she held the snake in place, with its tail thrashing around trying to free itself, Evan cut across its body, leaving the reptile in two pieces. Certain that they were safe, he took the mop handle from her, raising it slightly to make sure the rattler was dead. Satisfied, he dropped the mop, reaching for a crying Jean.

"Shhh, baby it's ok. You're safe now." Evan lifted her in his arms and carried her out of the kitchen into the great room, where he sat her down on the sofa. Jean shivered as if she were freezing cold. He feared she was going into shock. Holding her, Evan reached for the phone to call for help.

#

"What do you mean it was just one of those things?" Evan coarsely asked the police officer. He was furious. He was sure the snake had not wandered into the house on its own, but the officer disagreed. Evan and the officer were discussing the incident, while paramedics were finishing up with Jean.

"Sir, I think maybe it's one of your neighbor's pets that may have gotten loose. It happens all the time. It could have easily wandered in here through a door that was left open. You wouldn't believe some of the calls we get about stray pets of all kinds. Anywhere from runaway pigs to alligators. Just make sure from now on, all of your doors stay closed," the officer told him.

"Here, if you would just sign your statement…right here." The officer pointed at the signature line, after handing him the clipboard. Evan accepted the document, but not the cop's explanation. Signing his name he handed it back.

"Okay, sir. Animal control has disposed of the remains. Some soap and water and you will never know it was ever here. Smiling, the officer nodded at Jean before leaving, satisfied the incident was just an accident.

"Damn it! I don't buy it!"

Evan was angry. He thought he knew who may be responsible for the creepy crawly in Jean's kitchen— Nicolas. The man was none too happy when he threw him out. He may have been angry enough to get back at Jean for not reconciling.

"Honey, the officer could be right. It could just be someone's pet that had gotten out. I don't think Nicolas would be mad enough to do something like this. Besides, I don't think he has it in him.

After she and Evan had gotten in from a day of museums and a downtown music festival. She told Evan to wait in the upstairs lounge area, while she prepared dinner. She had gone into the kitchen to cook something quick, so they could have dinner on the oversized lounge sofa, followed by him as dessert.

She had just turned from pulling the pans she needed from the cupboard when she heard the rattling. Turning slowly, she spotted the snake not more than five feet from her. When she thought about her ordeal, Jean shivered.

"Are you ok? Do I need to call the paramedics back?" He asked her, drawing her tightly into his arms.

"No," she shook her head. "They said I was fine...I'm fine baby," she assured him, with a kiss. "Just hold me."

"Evan?"

"Hmm," he answered, rubbing her back.

"Do you think we could have dinner somewhere else?" She asked him. He nodded. "And Evan? Do you think we can spend the night somewhere else too?"

Smiling, Evan led her upstairs to pack. He was taking her home with him.

□

Chapter 10

Justin

Justin Graham sat in his custom-made leather chair, wondering why he hadn't been thrown out of his office. He was sure Anastasia would have contacted her team of lawyers by now to do just that. But he hadn't heard a peep out of her since he packed his bags and left his gilded cage. He would have bet money she would have at least shown up at his home to rant and threaten him, but he hadn't received even a phone call. This worried him. What was she planning? Would she go through with her previous threats to destroy him?

Justin had known the day would come when he would leave Anastasia, so he had planned well. He set up a separate account, stashing money for his planned escape. He had no intentions of leaving his hell of a marriage penniless. So when Anastasia did decide to rear her spiteful head, he was well prepared to start over fresh.

Putting Anastasia aside, he leaned back into his chair, propping his feet upon his desk. He thought about

Paige, his Paige. If he hadn't let his greed get in the way, she would be married to him and carrying his child, not Stone's.

He had come across them the night before while dining with a client. He and his guest had just been seated when he spotted them. He was a few tables away but made it a point not to be seen by either of them. What's more, if Anderson had caught sight of him, he would likely have made trouble for him. As he observed the couple, he could clearly see that Paige was pregnant. He had swallowed hard with regret. Justin was ashamed of the behavior he displayed when they were together. His greed had been his undoing.

Placing his feet on the floor again, he sat up, pounding his desk in frustration over the mistakes he made in dealing with Anastasia. And to make matters worse, mostly everything he had plotted upon, he was about to lose anyway, making his ill-gotten deals worthless.

"Mr. Graham?" His secretary asked from the intercom, bringing him back to reality.

"Yes, Meghan?" Justin thought he knew what this was about. He heard the hesitation in Meghan's voice. He assumed his wife had finally surfaced. Sighing he readied himself for the battle.

"There is a KT Ellis here to see you," Meghan told him.

Sighing again, this time with relief, he responded. "Send Mr. Ellis in."

"Mr. Graham…" Meghan started, only to be cut off by Justin.

"Meghan, just send him in," he demanded, not letting Meghan finish her sentence.

Justin shared with her that their days were numbered at Graham Inc. Even though his business was uncertain at the moment, he had every intention of starting a new company from scratch, hoping to bring most of his original staff along with him.

Ellis was a potential new hire. He made the appointment to meet with the new man before he decided to leave Anastasia. He was to be a replacement for his in-house investigator, Tor Hudson, who had left to start his private investigative firm. Under the circumstances, Justin just hoped he hadn't brought the new man in prematurely. He assumed Meghan was thinking the same.

Preparing to greet his guest, Justin stood, as his office door swung open. He was stopped short when his appointment entered, totally knocking him off guard. This was not who he expected. Hudson had recommended his top operative for his needs but failed to mention that the new *man* he expected was a woman.

Kaitlin Tamara Ellis, officially known as KT, stepped into the office, taking in the entire room in one glance. In her quick assessment, she surmised that Justin Graham was a hands-on executive. His desk was covered with various files and reports, unlike some administrators, whose titles were unearned, preferring to play golf instead of adequately running a business, leaving their administrative assistants to do all the work.

After sweeping the room, she brought her attention back to Justin, and from his expression, she was not what he expected. This part always amused KT. Men automatically assumed by her name and profession that she was male. Ignoring the questions displayed on his face, KT stepped forward to introduce herself.

"Mr. Graham, I'm KT Ellis." She didn't extend her hand, something Justin noted and wondered about.

"Ms. Ellis—"

"KT please," she interrupted, watching him intently.

"Okay then…KT, won't you have a seat?" Justin offered.

He was shocked. He couldn't quite get over the fact that Tor Hudson never mentioned the gender of the person he suggested when informing him of the investigator's qualifications. Quickly reflecting on their conversation, Justin realized, he assumed that KT was a man. What he did know, KT Ellis came highly recommended with excellent credentials, something he strongly required. He never in his wildest dreams expected a woman and a very attractive one at that, to fit those requirements. Justin made a mental note to reform himself of his misogynist way of thinking.

KT was at least five foot ten, slim, without an ounce of body fat. Although slender, he noticed she had curves where it counted. Her skin was a smooth sun-kissed honey brown. Her dark hair was cut in a short pixie style, perfectly complimenting her oval-shaped face.

Even though those attributes were appealing, the one thing that drew him most, was her piercing gray eyes; eyes that seemed to probe inside of him. She was dressed in black; black jeans, black shirt, and a black leather street vest. Her feet were clad in black low-heeled, leather boots. Her attire made him immediately think of a motorcycle and wondered if she owned one.

"KT," Justin corrected and continued, "I don't know how much Tor Hudson has told you about your assignments with my firm…"

"Tor told me everything that I needed to know, Mr. Graham. I understand you will need me for jobs that may be more difficult for some of your other operatives. That suits me just fine. I have been doing this type of work for quite some time, so it will not be a problem."

"I have looked over your proposed employment package and find it satisfactory," she continued. "I do have just one question. What is my first assignment?" KT never spent time beating around the bush. She found it annoying. The less time spent on small talk the better.

"This job may not be what you are accustomed to, but I need discretion in this matter," Justin informed her with a raised eyebrow. "I need you to find out what my soon-to-be ex-wife is up to."

Upon meeting KT, Justin decided he needed to find out just what Anastasia was planning. He concluded that surprises at this point weren't in his best interest. Especially since she had been uncomfortably quiet for quite some time now.

With KT being female, he felt this could work to his advantage. She would be able to get closer to Anastasia, better than any of his male employees. Besides, Anastasia knew those in his employ, since she handpicked most of them after they were married. Justin explained the circumstances involving his wife, and the need to resolve them as soon as possible

KT Ellis had accepted Justin Graham's assignment with a small frown. Part of her duties at Hudson's were to accept assignments outside the firm, with Graham Inc., and Stone Law Firm. This was her first outside assignment since joining Tor's organization.

KT was good at her job. She had been trained by the best—Tor Hudson himself. She had been a member of Tor's special-ops team in the army, accomplishing many tasks under his leadership. So when she decided to leave the military, Tor sought her out to become part of his investigative team. KT readily accepted. Like Tor, she loved her work but had grown weary of military life.

Making her way back downstairs to her waiting bike, she thought about her new employer. After the initial briefing and the perusal of the file he'd given her, she wondered if his wife was the woman he made her out to be.

In her experience, men tend to exaggerate when they are trying to get out from under a 'difficult' marriage. Most of the time, this creates an inaccurate description of the wife being the sole villain in the breakup.

Placing the file into the saddle bag, strapped to her black customized Ninja motorcycle, KT made a mental note to do some digging into Justin Graham's life, as well as his wife's. She didn't like surprises. She needed to get to know the players and what their motives were, to assess the job properly. Donning her helmet, she swung her leg over the bike's black leather seat, started the engine, and merged into traffic. She had work to do.

After KT accepted her assignment and left, Justin considered his newest employee. She wasn't very friendly, but neither was her mentor Tor Hudson. He wondered why the man failed to mention KT's gender. After some thought, he concluded that it didn't matter as long as she got the job done.

It had been over a week since he walked out on his wife and he hadn't heard from her. He hoped Ms. Ellis would be able to give him some answers soon because he needed to know what he was up against. Although Anastasia had threatened him on numerous occasions, he had never pushed her to the point of acting on those threats. At this point, he was undecided if she was capable of the follow-through. Justin leaned back into his chair. He would have to wait to find out.

Chapter 11

Jayden

Jayden Stone stared out the window of the coffee shop waiting for Hannah Pierce. He had gotten there early to grab his favorite booth in the back before the lunch crowd swarmed the place. It was a small diner with some of the best food in town, making it a very popular, but at times overly crowded place. He decided to wait for Hannah before ordering his favorite —chicken fried steak with a side of mashed potatoes and kale.

Jayden looked around when he heard his name. He saw the waitress point him out, at the inquiry of a woman. A woman he recognized immediately as the one he nearly knocked down in the airport. He stood as she made her way to his table.

Hannah was surprised to see the man who sent her bags skidding across the airport floor. She groaned as she walked towards his table. She never expected to see him again, let alone find him to be the subject of her article.

"Mr. Stone?" Hannah asked once she reached him.

"Ms. Pierce," Jayden acknowledged, gesturing towards the booth for her to sit. Before he could speak again, the helpful waitress appeared at their table. He wanted to apologize again, for knocking her over.

"Hi Jayden, will you be having your usual?" She asked.

"Yes, please. What would you like Ms. Pierce?" He asked Hannah.

"I don't think—" she began, only to be cut off by Jayden.

"We will both have the usual," he told the waitress. After placing their order, Jayden turned his attention to a fuming Hannah.

"Do you always take away people's choices as well as knock them down in airports?" She asked, clearly irritated.

Amused, Jayden sat back into the booth before he answered her. He could see she was still mad about the airport incident. He hoped to help her get over that.

Again, Jayden sized up the lovely Hannah Pierce. Her long, reddish brown hair was pulled into a loosely braided ponytail. He noticed the only make-up she wore was the shimmering caramel tint on her lips, highlighting her beautiful golden skin. Today she wore dark brown cotton slacks with a cream-colored, scooped-neck silk blouse. From her earlobes, hung shiny copper hoops, which sparkled from the light hanging over their table. On her right wrist, she wore a circle of multicolored wooden beads. He also noticed the absence of a ring on her left hand.

"I knew you were about to decline, so I ordered for you. I would like to make up for my clumsiness the other night at the airport. Please accept lunch as my small token of apology," he told her with a small smile. "That is, unless you rather I take you to dinner this evening instead?" He added.

Hannah stared at the arrogantly smug man sitting across from her. His eyes twinkled with amusement, while he awaited her answer. He is handsome she reflected, recalling her first encounter with him.

His perfectly shaped head was clean-shaven, the perfect complement to his high cheekbones and neatly trimmed mustache and goatee. She could see that he was fit. He would have to be, she surmised, because of his chosen field of work. How else would he have been able to rescue those children so effortlessly? This thought brought Hannah back to why she was there.

"Lunch will be just fine Mr. Stone," she conceded. "Now if we could get to the reason that I'm here," she told him, pulling her recorder and notepad from her handbag.

"Alright, but please call me Jayden," he said, with his smile widening. He noticed her frown was replaced with a faint smile of her own. Progress, he thought.

Reaching across the table, Hannah extended her hand. "Alright Jayden, you may call me Hannah." Still smiling, he shook her hand for a quick shake.

"Do you mind if I record our interview?" She felt the meeting would go smoothly if she didn't allow her initial feelings for this man to get in the way. Besides, after the interview, she didn't have to see him again.

#

Hannah left her meeting with Jayden perplexed. She thought she had him pegged, from the moment she first saw him. But coming away from the interview, he left her with questions. She had Jayden Stone pinned as a self-serving ass. However, after interviewing him, he came off as anything but. He seemed to be embarrassed by all of the attention he had gotten from his heroic deed. Hannah had expected him to have his chest stuck out; fishing for praise, but Jayden made it clear he was just performing his duties as a firefighter, nothing more.

While they talked and ate, she glimpsed a sadness that seemed to engulf him; a sadness he tried to hide behind his seemingly, playful remarks. Hannah got the impression that side of him was not who he was at all. It seemed forced; unnatural.

Even more puzzling, after their meeting, he shook her hand, paid for their meal, and left. Never once asking for her number or if he could see her again. A line she usually got from most of the single men she interviewed, whether they were involved or not. Hannah shook her head. She decided she wanted to know the real Jayden Stone.

#

Jayden ran through his workout routine, while he thought about his meeting with Hannah Pierce. He wanted to get to know her, but wasn't sure that he should, since his mind still dwelled on Andee. He knew she was lost to him forever, but he still loved her.

Finishing his last rep, he carefully replaced the weights he was using. Sitting up, he grabbed his towel from the floor, to wipe the sweat from his face and arms. Pitching the towel into a nearby chair, he prepared to do his lunges.

Hannah Pierce. Maybe he wrote her off too soon, he thought. Jayden shrugged. If it was meant to be, he would see her again. He would leave it up to the fates to settle that one. □

Chapter 12

Devin

Devin Powers paced the length of his friend Tor Hudson's office. He had just shared with him, his and Dani's break up. He and Tor had become friends after Tor married Dani's best friend Andee. Although he was closer to Anderson, another of Dani's friends, he felt Tor was the better choice to talk it out.

"She just left...just like that?" Tor asked of his friend. He could see that Devin loved her and was hurting. Tor hadn't known the couple that long, but he would have bet money Dani loved him as well, which made this turn of events difficult to understand.

Devin nodded. "She told me we shouldn't see each other anymore, grabbed her things, and left. I have been out of my mind. I have tried calling her...camping out at her house. Then yesterday, I got a call from Paige asking me what was going on. Dani left a note saying she was going away for a while. No explanation...nothing!" Devin was frustrated. He didn't know what to do.

"I came to you because I need to know that she's okay…not hurt or anything. Can you find her for me?" Devin asked.

Tor rubbed his chin. "Have you talked to her brother? Does he know where she is?'

"Dain knows she left. If he knows where she is, he's not saying," Devin informed him.

"I am sure I can find her…but man, if she doesn't want to be found, it may make things worse between you two."

Devin thought about what Tor was saying. He didn't want to push Dani away any further than he already had, but he needed to know she was safe.

"I'll tell you what. Find her just to make sure she's safe, that's all. You don't even have to tell me where she is. Will you do that much for me?"

Tor nodded.

Chapter 13

Anastasia

Anastasia walked into the lobby of Stan-Con Global. She looked around at the first-floor staff who tried their best to look anyway but curious. She assumed, by now, everyone had heard the news that her husband had left her.

Tilting her head higher, she strutted through the open lobby, as if she hadn't a care in the world. Although she looked unfazed on the outside, she was seething on the inside.

She still could not believe Justin had the balls to leave her. When she reached his suite of rooms and found that indeed his things were gone, she thought he would have a moment of sanity and would return. But it had been nearly two weeks and he was still gone. She had contemplated what to do about the situation. Her father had given his opinion, one she didn't want to hear—give the man a divorce and let him be.

Anastasia found herself in a dilemma. She had never had anyone to defy her; not a friend, family, and certainly not an employee. So it goes without saying that to have her husband leave her was monumental. She quickly dismissed her father's suggestion of a simple divorce. She would only give him one on her terms. That is if she chose to divorce him at all. At the moment, she hadn't decided on what she should do.

She called a meeting with her attorneys to weigh out her options. Aside from the prenuptial agreement she had him to sign, she never thought this far ahead. She was always assured that her money would keep him firmly in his place, under her rule.

Arriving at the board room, Anastasia threw her twenty thousand dollar handbag in a chair, and without preamble, fired off questions to her attorneys. Each one gave her legal ways of dealing with Justin. She was not interested in legal; she wanted revenge.

After her legal team left, Anastasia sat in one of the room's imported leather chairs. Her team had disappointed her with their legal this and compromise that. She wanted a different strategy. A strategy that would remind Mr. Justin Graham who was in control.

#

KT had watched Mrs. Stanton-Graham sashay through the lobby of the family corporation. She was there pretending to deliver a package to one of the many offices in the multi-storied building. This was her first time glimpsing the woman in the flesh. She noticed as Anastasia strolled through the lobby, most of the employees went out of their way not to make eye contact with the woman. KT wondered what that was all about. Making her way to the large circular information booth, in the middle of the lobby, she decided to ask some questions.

"May I help you?" The young, smartly dressed woman behind the desk asked her.

KT noticed the woman seemed relieved, after having watched Stanton-Graham enter the elevator.

"Yes, I'm not quite sure where I am supposed to deliver this," KT told the woman, as she handed her a package with its address purposely smudged. While the woman looked over the package, trying to make out the address, KT took this time to ask some questions.

"I loved the dress that woman was wearing. It looked as if it were made for her," she baited.

Forgetting the package for a moment, the woman took the bait. "It should look as if it were made for her, she probably spent a mint on it," the receptionist confided.

"Who is she anyway?" KT asked.

The woman lowered her voice and leaned forward. "Anastasia Stanton-Graham, soon to be Anastasia Stanton again. The cow that owns this place," the receptionist told her while cutting her eyes around the lobby. She wanted to make sure she wasn't overheard.

"Wow, it sounds like there is a divorce in her future," KT pressed further.

With eyes darting around again, before leaning in even closer, the woman confided more. "And it couldn't be happening to a meaner bitch," she spat, before handing the package back to KT.

"Here hon, this address is in the next block up," she told her. "And be grateful you didn't have to deliver anything to the wicked witch. She has been particularly nasty since her husband left her. If you ask me, he shouldn't have married that terror in the first place."

Getting what she needed, KT bid the woman a good day and left. Once outside, KT tossed the package into the nearest trash bin. Its job was done.

So, Anastasia Stanton-Graham was the bitch her husband made her out to be. This made KT more curious as to why Justin married her, to begin with. She had to have been the same woman before he married her, so what was his purpose? Sighing, she realized she had more digging to do. She was just about to hail a cab, when she spotted a silver Range Rover, pulling up to the curb.

The man who climbed out was short, overweight, and dressed in a brown velour jogging suit. KT thought those things were killed off in the eighties. Curious, she watched the man shuffle through the glass doors of Stan-Con Global.

Stepping to the wall of glass doors to look inside, she watched him as he made his way to the information desk. Certain that he had to be in the wrong building, KT was surprised when the receptionist greeted him as if she knew him. They seemed to exchange pleasantries before the man waddled off to the elevator. She wondered what type of dealings this man, who was clearly into the shadiest of businesses, could have in that building.

Stepping back to the curb, KT noted the out-of-state license plate and jotted it into a small notebook she always kept on her. This job was more tangled than she suspected. The vehicle was registered in Justin Graham's home state. The thug may or may not have anything to do with her assignment, but she had to find out more to be sure.

☐

Chapter 14

Dani

Dani Sinclair sat in her comfortable compartment on a train headed to Toronto, Canada via the scenic route. Not in any hurry to arrive at her destination, she chose this mode of travel to think. She needed time to reflect on what had transpired between her and Devin, and why she couldn't marry him. She never thought her past actions would cost her a good relationship.

Dani stared out the window at the passing scenery, not actually seeing it at all. Her mind was too full of yesteryears and the choices she made. If only she could go back and change things; make things right. She sighed. There was no coming back from this, no matter how much she wished.

Still gazing back on her past, Dani heard a slight knock on her compartment door. She politely allowed the attendant to enter. She had been on the train for a full twenty-four hours and had declined dinner the night before. She assumed it was an attendant from the dining car.

"Ms., I wanted to inform you that I can bring breakfast if you would like," the attendant told her.

Not having eaten since she boarded the train, she thought it wise to have breakfast. She didn't want to be sick on top of everything else. Having given the attendant her breakfast order, Dani rose to slip into her private bath to wash her hands. But before she could accomplish this, there was another knock on the door.

"Ms. Sinclair, I hate to ask this of you, but we're about to pull into the station in Chicago, and running to full capacity. I was told to ask if you would mind sharing your compartment for the last leg of the trip?" The previous attendant asked her.

Dani sighed. Her whole purpose of the trip was for solitude with much meditation. But if the room was needed, she didn't see why she couldn't share her space. They were to arrive in Toronto late evening, so sleeping arrangements wouldn't be an issue.

Maybe she could use the company. No amount of thinking was going to change the situation anyway. She agreed to share her space when they stopped in Chicago. She just hoped it wasn't with some talkative shrew or some other annoying person, who would make her regret her decision.

Just as she finished her breakfast, the train pulled into the station. She watched various passengers move to and fro on the platform. Dani tried to imagine the person who would join her from the people she saw passing her window. Not knowing who she was looking for, she finally gave up, deciding to read a book from her Kindle instead. Soon there was another tap on her compartment door.

"Come in," she told the person without looking up from her book. She only glanced up, when she heard the door slide open.

Her eyes started their assessment from the stranger's feet and worked their way up his body to his face. Once she reached his face her brow rose. He was not what she was expecting. She assumed her compartment mate would be a woman and at the very least a middle-aged woman. What stood before her was a woman's dream.

"Ms. Sinclair…is it?" The man asked. Dani could only nod. Coming fully into the small room, the man swung his backpack from his shoulder, placing it, along with a carry-on, on a nearby table.

"Hi, I guess I'm your guest until we reach Toronto," the man said. "Oh, and by the way, my name is Maalik Wyatt," he told her with a smile and an outstretched hand.

Lifting her eyes from his body, Dani placed her hand in his, as he firmly shook it.

"Nice to meet you Maalik…call me Dani, please," she told him, as he released her hand and sat down.

"I hope I am not intruding," Maalik said, pulling his iPad from his backpack. "I had to catch this train at the last minute. I missed my flight to Toronto, and the next one out wasn't until tomorrow morning. I needed to be in Toronto by the time I would have been boarding the flight. So I decided since I could get there this evening by train…," he shrugged, trailing off.

"It's not a problem. If I were honest with myself, I was getting a little stir-crazy, being isolated from the other passengers, so welcome Maalik." Dani smiled.

"Thank you."

Tapping his iPad on, Maalik, pulled up his email account. Tapping rapidly over the keypad, he tapped out a single sentence, before hitting send—**I'm with her**. Satisfied that his boss would be relieved, he logged off, placing the tablet back into his backpack.

"So Dani, is your trip business or pleasure?" Maalik asked with a knowing smile.

#

Tor Hudson closed his eyes with a sigh of relief. His operative had found Dani. And since he didn't add anything to the short message, he knew she was safe. At least he could tell his friend that much. Maalik was to stay with Dani as long as he was needed.

After running some checks on her credit cards, Tor found she was headed to Canada. He had his man fly to Chicago to meet her train. Tor had already made arrangements to have Maalik seated in her compartment. He called in some favors from an ex-military man who was an employee of the railway line.

Now all he had to do was wait. This part would be easy for him, but he doubted if it would be for Devin. Although he said he didn't want to know where she was, only to know she was safe, Tor knew once Devin discovered he knew her whereabouts that would change.

Sighing again, Tor picked up the phone to call his friend. He would persuade him to let him do his job and not interfere. He liked Devin and Dani. He hoped they could work out their differences. But that may not happen, if Devin decided to track her down, which is precisely what he predicted he would do if he were to discover her location.

Tor brought his mind back to the present when his call connected. "I've found her and she's safe," he told an anxious Devin. Now comes the hard part, he thought.

Chapter 15

Hannah

Hannah concentrated, as she hurriedly typed the article's last sentences. Her fingers flew over the keyboard, adding the finishing touches that would wrap up her piece on Jayden Stone. She still marveled over the man's ability to catch the little boy who leaped from the window of the burning building.

After the interview, she discovered someone in the crowd had videoed the incident, and it had gone viral across the internet. Hannah had watched the scene a few times herself. She noticed the ease with which Jayden caught the boy.

Since her time with Jayden, she had become more intrigued with the man. Despite her misgivings at the start of the meeting, she wanted to know more about the man himself, not just the hero that played out on the six o'clock news. Something about him called to her. He seemed troubled over something. She felt in him a kindred spirit.

After running the article through the proofreading software, Hannah emailed it to her editor, to be included in the next issue of the magazine. She looked at the clock and realized she had made the deadline by thirty minutes. The magazine was due out in the next couple of days. Hannah wasn't sure she could wait that long before contacting Jayden. She told him she would let him know when the magazine hit the newsstands. Going against her better judgment, she picked up her phone to call him.

#

Hannah Pierce had decided to move, after running into her last romantic encounter, in one of her favorite restaurants. Even though they were no longer dating, seeing him was still a harsh reminder of her poor sense of judgment.

She met Dain Sinclair on one of her trips to cover a story. He had been the pilot on her flight, where he noticed her boarding and asked her out before leaving the aircraft. They had dated off and on over a couple of years. She thought the off element of their relationship was due to their busy schedules; him flying here and there, and her with her job assignments taking her from place to place.

She had known from the beginning he wasn't the commitment type, but she thought they had a good thing that would eventually lead to something solid. She should have known better, but her heart had gotten in the way and had blinded her to what was going on.

Out of the two years they were seeing each other, Hannah had never been to Dain's home. He always stayed over at her place. They went out in public occasionally but never did the things that most couples enjoyed together.

At first, she thought he was hiding a wife, but soon found that wasn't true. She told herself, he was just being cautious; afraid of being the one left hurt. Hannah loved him and waited patiently for him to realize she was there to stay. She had revealed how she felt and assumed because he continued to see her, he had accepted her love and wanted a serious relationship also. Especially after receiving a few whispered 'I love you's from him. However, she could never have been more wrong.

After a few months of a hot and heavy romance, with her love for him displayed willingly and openly, he abruptly stopped calling and coming around. At first, she thought he may have been busy. Heaven knows she had her moments when her job had overwhelmed her. But one day, when she happened to be out running errands, she ran into him with another woman. He simply explained that their time had run its course, and he reminded her that he didn't do commitments. And just like that, he was out of her life.

Hannah was devastated. She had given Dain her love and time, only to be shoved aside for the next conquest. She had gone home that day to lick her wounds and grieve. She knew she should have been smarter when it came to a man like Dain, but she had fooled herself into believing, that if he hadn't left after she made her feelings clear, he was there to stay. She couldn't believe he had used her emotions to his advantage. He didn't care that she loved him and he certainly didn't love her.

Not long after, she stumbled upon an announcement that he was engaged to the woman whom she had seen him in the restaurant with. The same woman she had warned about him. After that heartbreaking blow, Hannah felt it was time she stepped up her plans to make her move from Metro City. The place where she had spent the majority of her life.

So here she was, in a new city, a new state. It was past time that she got on with her life. A life that was free of everything Dain Sinclair.

#

"Hey Stone, you have a call," one of Jayden's coworkers called out to him.

Jayden hoped everything was ok. Normally when he got a call at the firehouse, it was on his cell.

"Hello, this is Jayden," he told the caller. Not getting an immediate answer, he was about to hang up when Hannah spoke,

"Jayden…Hannah Pierce here, how are you?" She asked, trying to keep the nervousness from her voice. She almost hung up after hearing his voice, feeling she'd made a mistake in contacting him. She could have easily sent him an email about the article.

"I'm good, how about you?" He asked, glad she had called. He had been thinking about her since the interview.

"I'm great. I just sent your article in and it should be on the stands the day after tomorrow. I just wanted to let you know. And I wanted to thank you again for granting me the interview." Hannah hoped she sounded professional. She didn't want him to think she had called to hear his voice.

"Thanks for letting me know. Although, I don't know if I should tell my coworkers since they have been dragging me ever since they found out about the interview. They know what a private person I am. I hope your article reflects that," he told her.

"Of course. You don't have to worry about that. It just gives the details of your actions in rescuing the kids. Unlike some others in my profession, I understand perfectly about personal space and privacy. I think you will be very pleased, once you read it." Hannah smiled. She found herself wanting to please this man.

"Well, I just wanted to thank you again and give you the information. I will let you get back to what you were doing," Hannah said. She thought she had taken up enough of his time.

"Wait!" Jayden told her, fearing she would hang up before he asked her out. "Hannah, I would like to see you again, if it's not asking too much. I know you probably get this all the time, but I just would like a little dinner and some conversation that's all. If the answer is no, I will understand." Jayden held his breath, while he waited for her answer.

"No Jayden, it's not asking too much. Take down my number. I will be out of town for a couple of days on assignment. Give me a call later in the week and we can make a date," she told him. She was relieved that he asked her out. Hannah gave him the number and hung up pleased. She was anxious to see him again.

Jayden placed the phone back onto the cradle with a grin. "So fate did step in." He would get that chance to know Hannah Pierce.

☐

Chapter 16

Dani

Dani laughed as Maalik told her stories from his childhood. She hadn't laughed in days and it felt good.

Her compartment mate was charming and very funny. She thought he was wasting his time as an 'ad executive'. He could easily have done standup comedy. Wiping her eyes at his latest story, she held up her hand.

"Maalik," she said still laughing, "you have to stop before I bust a gut. Man, you are hilarious. Have you ever tried stand-up? I think you would be a natural." Dani truly liked him. They had spent a few hours together talking and getting to know each other. He had taken her mind off of her troubles.

"Nah...I don't think that's in me. I would probably have instant stage fright trying to tell my stories in front of a bunch of people," he told her shaking his head.

Maalik found he liked Dani, a lot. She was easy to talk to and easy on the eyes. He didn't know much about this assignment. Only that she and the boyfriend had a disagreement and he was worried about her. He wanted her followed to make sure she stayed safe.

Hmm, he thought, too bad she had a man. He could see himself with a woman like Dani. Still, if at the end of the job, and things didn't work out between her and the boyfriend...who knows?

"How about we go to the dining car for dinner, and stretch our legs? What do you say?" He asked her.

Maalik and Dani had been talking nonstop, since Maalik's arrival. They were having such a good time, they had lunch brought to them, instead of joining the other passengers in the dining room.

"Sure, why not," Dani agreed. She preceded him into the corridor and waited, while he locked their compartment. They made small talk as they made their way to the dining car.

While they ate, Dani told him about her family. She shared that she, and her twin brother Dain, were the only ones left after their parents died in a car crash. She found him easy to talk to. More so, because she knew once they reached Toronto, they would part ways, becoming strangers again.

While Maalik talked, she took note of the handsome man. He was tall and athletically built. His black hair was cropped close to his head. She let her eyes travel over smooth brown skin, which looked to be well-maintained. His silken mustache and brows, along with the jawline of a warrior, made him appear sensitive, yet strong. She noticed too, that he had lashes most women would kill for.

They were just finishing dinner when the train slowed to a crawl and then stopped. It was dusk outside and all they could see were miles and miles of flat land.

"I wonder what's going on," Dani said more to herself than Maalik.

"Although I haven't ridden a train since I was a kid, I would think it couldn't be too much. It's probably nothing," he assured her.

Just as he was finishing his sentence, a voice came over the intercom, informing them that a freight train had overturned, due to a collision with a stalled vehicle a few miles up the track. They were nearly a hundred miles from the nearest city and would have to wait for the wreck to be removed and the track inspected for damage before they could continue. At that time, it was not known how long the delay would be before the train could continue to its destination.

"Oh my God, I hope no one was hurt," Dani whispered. Although she wanted to reach her destination, she wasn't in any hurry to get there. Then she remembered Maalik's meeting in Toronto.

"Oh no, Maalik, your meeting..." She knew he had avoided one delay that day, and now here he was stuck on the train.

Maalik sighed. "Well, there is nothing I can do about the accident. If we aren't cleared to continue in time for me to make the meeting, the company will just have to understand and I'm sure they will, once I explain. I can conduct my business later or another day." He shrugged.

Unbeknownst to Dani, she was his business. Where ever she went, he was sure to follow, until Tor called him off. He would just have to make the best of it. He hid a grin behind his napkin, as he wiped his mouth. He would happily extend the trip, if it meant he would get to spend more time with Dani.

#

"Are you comfortable?" Dani asked Maalik.

They had made their way back to their room. Before they left the dining car, they were informed by staff, it would probably be morning before the mess was cleared. Having no other choice, they would have to bunk together.

"Yes, I'm fine. Are you sure you don't want the bottom bunk?" He asked her.

She had just come in from changing into some shorts and a tee shirt. He had donned a pair of athletic shorts and had gotten into his bunk, while she was gone.

"No, the top is fine," she told him.

Remembering he should check in, Maalik climbed from his bed to grab his iPad, just as Dani turned from putting her things away. They collided. Pinned against the counter, Dani found herself pressed firmly against Maalik.

Neither one said anything or moved. Dani let her gaze travel from his bare chest to his mouth. Maalik placed his hands on her slender waist, as he lowered his mouth towards hers. Dani closed her eyes, while she waited for his lips to reach hers.

Locking his lips onto hers, Maalik kissed her softly at first, anticipating resistance. Feeling none, he strengthened the kiss, parting her lips with his tongue. Maalik moaned as he pulled her closer to him. His erection let her know what he wanted. He wanted this woman. He wanted her in the worst way. Mentally coming to his senses, he knew he couldn't have her. He was there to do a job and not to seduce his charge.

Reluctantly pulling away, Maalik set her away from him, apologizing as he did so. This was so unlike him. He had never let a pretty face get in the way of his job, not once; not until tonight. Tor trusted him and he couldn't betray that trust. Not only was Tor his boss, but his best friend. Swallowing hard, he helped her into her bunk and turned out the light, before getting into his own bed.

Dani lay in her bed trying to pull herself together. She was very much attracted to the man who lay just beneath her, and hadn't wanted him to stop. It was just as well. Even though she was no longer with Devin, sleeping with Maalik would not have solved anything.

She half smiled. Maalik was a true gentleman. Any other man would have taken her without a second thought. She respected him for that. He would make some woman a wonderful husband, she thought. Turning over, she closed her eyes, as a single tear traveled down her cheek. She missed Devin.

#

Dani came awake with the movement of the train. She sat up and stretched. Peering out the window, she saw that it was a rainy day. At least they were on their way again. Closing her eyes, she thought about what almost happened the night before with Maalik. Dani touched her lips, as she recalled the kiss that had her wanting more. Her body reacted just thinking about it.

Remembering Maalik, she looked down at his bunk to find it empty. Bounding from her bed, she tapped on the bathroom door.

"Maalik?" No answer. She knew he was near because his belongings were still there. Shrugging, Dani gathered her things, and let herself into the bath for a shower.

After showering and dressing, she emerged from the bathroom to find Maalik had righted the bunks and had placed breakfast on the table. She also noticed he had showered and changed.

"Good morning. I hope you slept well. I got up early, and showered down the way, in one of the public baths. I didn't want to disturb you," he told her. "As you can see, I got us breakfast," he gestured to the spread.

"Maalik, about last night," Dani started. She held up her hand, sensing he was about to interrupt her.

"No let me finish," she told him. "Maalik, I like you and I would not have stopped you had you taken it further. I don't know your relationship status, other than you said you weren't married. But me, I just broke up with my boyfriend and…well, even though I did want you, it may not have been wise for me to fall into bed with you. What I'm trying to say is, that you did nothing wrong, you have nothing to apologize for. We were two consenting adults so…" she trailed off not knowing how to end that sentence.

Maalik was relieved. He considered Dani a friend and hoped there wouldn't be any awkwardness between them. He had already chastised himself most of the night, for putting her in that situation in the first place. Now hearing she wanted him too, let him off the hook a little. Although, he knew he should never have kissed her to start with.

"Dani, I consider you a friend and I hoped I hadn't messed that up, by what happened last night. If you can let it go, so can I. Agreed?" He asked her with an outstretched hand.

"Agreed," Dani approved, placing her hand in his for a shake. Now let's eat this wonderful food you've brought, shall we?"

They ate and talked like old friends, never once mentioning the previous night's adventures.

#

"Well, I guess this is where we say goodbye," Maalik told Dani, after they exited the train, onto the platform. They had finally reached their destination. "I want to thank you for sharing your compartment with me," he added.

"Anytime," Dani told him with a chuckle. "I hope your business here goes well," she continued. She was reluctant to let him go. Although she knew they would part, she suddenly found herself not wanting to.

"Maalik, how long do you plan to be in Toronto?" She suddenly asked him.

"Oh, I don't know, a couple of days. Why?"

"Well, I don't know if you have plans or not, but how about later, after your meeting, you come to join me for a late dinner tonight? I would welcome the company," she told him, hoping he would accept.

Maalik pretended to mull this over. This would solve the problem of him having to skulk around to follow her. If she were with him… "Sure why not," he accepted.

They made plans to meet later in the lobby of her hotel. They would decide where to go for dinner from there. In the meantime, this would allow him the opportunity to size up the situation and check in with Tor. He was still puzzled by her comment about being unattached.

Chapter 17

Justin

Justin maneuvered his way into traffic, after a long
tense day. Tense, because he still hadn't heard from
Anastasia. It had been three days since he hired KT to find
out what she was up to, and still nothing. KT had reported
that his wife had not left North Carolina. This puzzled him.
If she wasn't going to do her dirty work herself, he was
sure he would have heard from her lawyers by now.

Deciding not to take the surface streets home, he
made his way to the freeway on ramp, pushing the car's
speed to merge safely with the flowing traffic. He had just
merged into the second lane when he spotted tail lights,
indicating traffic was slowing down.

Justin sighed. He thought he had waited long
enough for rush hour to be over, before heading home.
Pressing his brakes to slow his Mercedes, he found he had
no brakes. Trying not to panic, he pressed them again, only
to get the same response, no brakes. Quickly glancing into
each of his mirrors for nearby cars, he had to make a

decision. If he were to crash, he didn't want to take anyone along with him. Finding the lane to his right open, he steered the car into it, praying he could stop it somehow.

Once reaching the far right lane, he had no choice but to continue to steer the car onto the shoulder and down the embankment, to avoid hitting other motorists. Bracing himself, he headed for a tangle of brush and trees that brought the car to an abrupt stop. Raising his left arm to shield himself from the oncoming airbag, Justin felt his forearm snap, as the force of the bag hit him. Writhing in pain, he hadn't realized some of the commuters had stopped to help him.

"Hey buddy, are you alright?" A man asked him. He motioned for Justin to unlock the door. Once the door was unlocked, the man pulled the driver's side door open. He had been driving behind Justin when he suddenly veered off the road. The man immediately pulled over to help. Soon others joined him, wanting to know if he needed an ambulance.

The bystanders helped Justin out of the car. The first man helped him to sit on the side of the embankment until help arrived.

"Man that was some accident. What happened? He asked Justin.

Cradling his broken arm, he gritted his teeth. "My brakes went out," he told the good Samaritan. "I was just driving along and…my brakes were just gone."

He laid back on the ground, trying to calm himself. He wondered why the brakes failed. His first thought was of Anastasia. Could she have done something like this? He had just had his car serviced a few weeks ago and there hadn't been any problems. This, coupled with not hearing from her, put her involvement at the top of his list of suspicions.

Asking the man his name, he asked Joseph, if he would retrieve his phone from his car. Taking it with his good hand, Justin dialed KT. She answered on the first ring. Without a preamble, Justin informed her that someone had just tried to kill him.

#

KT closed her phone with a snap. She didn't like this turn of events. Justin Graham believed someone had tried to kill him. She was sitting outside of Stan-Con Global, waiting for Anastasia to emerge. She had been following the woman for the past few days, but nothing had turned up. The woman hadn't even made a phone call that was out of the ordinary.

KT frowned. If Mrs. Stanton-Graham was behind Justin's crash, she had someone working for her and was communicating with this person other than the normal modes of communication. At any rate, she needed to make it back to Justin. It seemed all the excitement was at his end.

Dropping her coffee cup into the trash, and hoisting her backpack onto her shoulder, KT raised her hand to summon a taxi. Climbing into the cab, she gave the driver her destination—the airport. She, like Justin, didn't think it was a coincidence that his brakes suddenly failed without warning. Considering the circumstances, the timing was just too convenient. It screamed deliberate. She had to get back before someone made another attempt on Justin's life.

☐

Chapter 18

Evan

Evan watched Jean swim the length of his heated indoor pool. He had just arrived home from the office. It had been a few days since the snake incident and Jean had finally started to relax. He hated having to leave her alone, but he had a meeting with board members, which he could not skip. Besides, he knew she was safe in his home in San Francisco. He lived in a gated community, where no one gained entrance without authorization.

Deciding to join her in her swim. Evan quickly removed his tie, shirt, and undershirt, tossing them on a nearby table. Kicking out of his hand-made shoes, he removed his socks, trousers, and underwear. Completely nude, he dove into the pool, startling Jean.

"Evan, I didn't know you were home," she told him, recovering from her fright. Swimming towards him, she splashed water at him for scaring her.

"I'm sorry babe, you looked so peaceful, I didn't want to disturb you." Pulling her to him for a kiss, Evan guided her hand to his erect penis.

Jean smirked. "Where are your swim trunks sir?" she asked him playfully. She slowly slid her hand along his shaft, while they tread water. She watched as his eyes changed from a caramel brown to a smoky dark brown.

"I think the question is, why do you have these clothes on?" He unhooked her bikini top, releasing it to float away. Next, he helped her out of her bottom.

Now that they were both naked, Jean wrapped her legs around his waist, and he entered her. Although she had been the one to postpone their intimacy from the start, Evan was glad they waited. This gave them each time to be tested for STIs and gave Jean time to take care of birth control, eliminating their need for condoms.

Jean gasped, as Evan began thrusting inside of her. She had never made love in a pool before but found that she enjoyed it. They had drifted to the side of the pool, where Evan braced himself, driving deeper.

Wanting more of her, with Jean still wrapped around him, Evan walked up the tiled steps, out of the pool, to a nearby chaise. Turning her over onto her knees, he entered her from behind, continuing their lovemaking, with both crying out in ecstasy. Climaxing, Evan exploded inside of her, leaving both of them spent.

Switching places with her, Evan pulled Jean on top of him. Finally bringing his breathing under control, Evan whispered to a dozing Jean, "Marry me."

Chapter 19

Jayden

Dressed to make an impression, Jayden stood outside Hannah's door. He wore navy slacks paired with a causal tieless Brooks Brother's shirt. His black handmade leather shoes were polished to perfection. They made plans to drive to Jackson for dinner. A forty-five-minute drive that would give them time to talk and get to know each other. The restaurant he chose, boasted rave reviews for their dinner menu.

Although he was still smarting from Andee's marriage, Jayden believed the only way to put the pain behind him was to move on. Besides, he liked Ms. Pierce. He found her appealing, even when she was mad at him for knocking her down.

"It's now or never," he muttered to himself, before ringing her bell. He rocked on his heels while he waited for her to answer.

Hannah was giving her reflection a final inspection when the doorbell chimed. She had chosen a sea-foam green halter-styled dress with floral prints of reds, purples, and a deeper green. She had spent the afternoon getting her hair and nails done for the occasion. Usually, she wore her long hair straight but opted for curls for her night out with Jayden. She didn't know why she was so hyped by a simple dinner. It wasn't like she hadn't had dinner dates before. Checking her reflection once more, she moved to answer the door.

"Hi Jayden, won't you come in? I will only be a minute." She stepped aside to allow him entrance.

Closing the door behind him, she offered him a seat while she retrieved her purse and shawl. Jayden watched the sway of her hips as she sashayed into the other room. He wondered when he would get to see those hips uncovered. Grimacing, he quickly chastised himself. He barely knew the woman, and here he was already undressing her.

"Ok, I'm ready." Jayden escorted her to his car.

#

"Wow, the food is really good. The folks at the magazine were right," Hannah commented on her entrée. She had chosen lamb chops with scalloped potatoes and grilled asparagus with a rich hollandaise sauce. She took a sip from her wine glass.

Nodding, Jayden agreed. "I must say, I've had roasted pork many ways, but this is by far the best," he told her before taking another bite of his meal.

The restaurant was rustic, but upscale just the same. Jayden understood why they needed to make reservations. The room only held a total of ten dining tables, which made their visit more intimate. They learned, upon arriving, that the restaurant was only open for a certain number of hours a day and only for those who had reservations. It was well worth the trip.

"So I guess we both have something in common," Hannah remarked, after cutting into her lamb. They were discussing why she picked up and moved. She confided that she was sort of running away from bad memories of a failed relationship. She told Jayden about her misreading of her last one.

"Well, yeah I guess you can say that," he nodded. "But the failure was all my own doing, in my relationship." He told her about his foolish mistakes with Andee.

"And mine wasn't? I fooled myself into believing I *had* a relationship," she told him, shaking her head in disgust.

Jayden shook his head in disagreement. "That wasn't all your doing. Any man who would stick around, knowing there was no future, especially after you proclaimed your love for him, is an ass, to say the least. He's a user and a manipulator for sure."

Jayden couldn't believe there were supposedly grown men, still running around playing games with women's hearts. This brought him back to Dain and Taylor. He just hoped Dain didn't hurt his cousin.

"You know when I first met you, I had you pegged to be just such a guy. I'm glad I was wrong," Hannah confessed. "And before you go all off on me, in my defense, I was still smarting from relationship pain and had pretty much painted all men with the same brush."

"One thing is for sure my lady; you can never accuse me of being 'that guy'. Besides, my mother would kill me." They both laughed.

"If you like, we can stop in on a jazz club I know that's nearby. They have great music. What do you say?" Jayden wanted to spend more time with her. He enjoyed being with her.

"I say yes."

They finished their dinner and then drove to the club, where they had drinks and listened to the live band.

#

"I had a great time Jayden," Hannah told him as they walked to her door. It was late when they made it back to her apartment. "Would you like to come in?"

"No, it's late. But I will give you a call later. Maybe we can plan something for later in the week."

Jayden smiled. Hannah was fun to be with. He discovered not only was she beautiful and smart, she was witty. He found her very appealing. Pulling her to him, Jayden kissed her softly on the cheek. Touching her chin, he smiled then left.

Hannah closed her door after watching him drive away. She smiled. Jayden was a true gentleman. She touched her cheek before heading to bed.

Chapter 20

Maalik

Maalik and Dani had gotten back to her hotel just after midnight.

Before leaving for dinner, Maalik confided he lost his hotel reservation, because of the train delay. He told Dani, he had forgotten to call ahead, to request they hold his room. And because there were several conventions in the city, he was unable to secure another one for the night. Dani had quickly offered the extra bed. She didn't see why it would be a problem, considering they shared a room the night before; though neither brought up what happened between them in that room.

While he waited for the appointed time to meet her for dinner, Maalik checked in with Tor. He let him know he had everything under control. He explained about the delay and told him he would make sure Dani Sinclair stayed safe.

Maalik didn't tell Tor about the night's sleeping arrangements. He had purposely let his room go, so he could move in with Dani. He knew once she heard his tale of woe, she would allow him to room with her. He told himself, it was because he wanted to make his job easier. But if that were true, why hadn't he mentioned his plans to Tor?

Riding the elevator up to their floor, Maalik thought over their conversation at dinner. He casually mentioned her breakup, where he discovered Dani, and her ex Devin, were done. She didn't go into much detail only to say they would never get back together. He wanted to ask Tor about the circumstances surrounding Dani and Devin but felt he could not do so, without arousing Tor's suspicions that he was up to something.

He wasn't…was he? Pushing that thought from his mind, he held the door open for Dani to exit the elevator.

Yawning Dani slipped out of her shoes the moment they entered the room. She was tired.

"Choose either bed Maalik, I am going to take a hot shower and climb under the covers. Yawning again, she gathered her things and went into the bathroom.

Maalik placed his backpack and tote on the bed nearest the door. He retrieved his things from the front desk where he stored them, until after they returned from dinner.

Looking at the chained door, he still felt he needed to be near it, just in case some intruder entered the room unexpectedly. Maalik pulled his pajama bottoms from his bag along with his toothbrush and other toiletries.

He sat on his bed waiting for his turn in the bath. He wondered about his motives for being in Dani's room. Were they as pure as he tried to lead himself to believe? Drawing his hand down his face, he felt he was overthinking the situation. Besides, if something were to happen, like she said, they were two consenting adults. Neither were attached at the moment. So what could be the harm?

When the shower stopped, Maalik rose and stepped out into the hallway to take a look around. He knew this assignment was not dangerous, but old habits die hard. Besides, he needed to clear his head. He made a deal with himself. If it came down to them falling into bed together he would stop only if she wanted him to. There would be no regrets.

Stepping back into the room, he found only the entryway light on. Dani had climbed into bed and was asleep. Taking this as a sign, Maalik sighed, gathered his things, and stepped into the bathroom. He would be taking a cold shower tonight.

☐

Chapter 21

Justin

"So what did you find concerning the car?" Justin asked KT.

She had flown back to town as soon as she could, to get to the bottom of his accident. Pushing her initial suspicions aside, she wanted to believe it was just a mechanical error that caused the crash. But after speaking with the mechanic, who she had to check out the car, she had to admit Justin was correct. Someone was out to kill him. His brake line had been tampered with.

"The brake line had been cut," she told him.

"I knew it! That bitch is trying to have me killed! I knew when I didn't hear from her, she was up to something. But I must admit, I didn't think even she would go this far." Justin was beside himself. He thought his wife would have taken legal actions against him, not his life.

Justin tried to rise from his chair to grab his laptop. This task was made difficult due to his broken arm and sore body from the crash.

"So we have to find the person she's hired to do the job," he told KT.

"Hold up buddy, 'we' aren't going to do anything. That's my job, remember? You need to rest."

KT was not about to let him get involved with the investigation. He was too close to it to be effective. Besides, she worked better alone.

Justin fell back into his chair. "Suppose she tries again? I doubt if she will stop until I'm dead," he told her.

"Someone will be with you at all times. I haven't lost a client and I am not about to start."

Pausing a minute, KT had to know. "If I may ask. Why did you marry that woman in the first place?" She dug up as much as she could on the subject but was unable to get an answer. Whatever the reason, nobody was talking. So what better way to get the answer than from the man himself?

Justin was uneasy at first. Only a few people knew the true circumstances behind his and Anastasia's marriage. Her parents didn't even know. He guessed it didn't really make much difference now that he was trying to sever ties with the vindictive bitch. Inhaling deeply, he explained the entire disastrous mess.

Justin expelled a ragged breath. "I played a game, to which I didn't understand the rules," he started.

Justin went on to tell her about his plan to seduce Anastasia, to obtain lucrative contracts for his business. He explained the consequences that resulted from that plan, which led him to lose the woman he loved and his freedom.

"And to top it all off, I made a fool of myself by following Paige and Stone to Aruba, which resulted in me being arrested. Stone and I had a little altercation in their hotel room, after their very public engagement in one of the island's most exclusive restaurants. Now you know my shame," he concluded.

KT heard everything he confessed but chose to dwell on Anastasia's motives. "So, she got pregnant purposely to get you to marry her?" Justin nodded.

"After what happened yesterday, I very much believe she would have ruined you if you hadn't," KT agreed. "The hunter became the game." She said more to herself than Justin. She knew from experience how things can turn on a dime.

"That's about the gist of it," he told her. Justin cringed to think what Anastasia would have done had he not married her. Would she have targeted Paige? He shook his head at his stupidity.

"Excuse me a moment." KT stepped outside to make a call.

\#

Tor hung up the phone, ending the conversation with KT. She brought him up to date on the Graham case. It appeared Anastasia Graham had upped the ante on the whole mess. Tor figured this would be a nasty divorce, but to try and have the man killed?

Thinking about what their next move should be, Tor sighed. When he started his agency, it was to delegate assignments and not to have to work them himself. But since he was just getting started and only had a handful of employees, he would have to get involved. Someone needed to work the investigation, while KT kept an eye on Justin. She couldn't be in two places at once.

Picking up the phone again, he made flight reservations to Raleigh, North Carolina. He had to get there as soon as possible to stop Anastasia from taking his client out. With that done, Tor shook his head. Now he would have to tell his wife that dinner plans would have to wait.

#

Roland Stanton walked into his daughter's darkened bedroom. Miss Allison had called him after she couldn't get her to eat anything. Anastasia had been holed up in her suite since the day before. It was unlike her not to perform as Lady of the Manor, ordering everyone around, not even for one day.

"Anastasia?" Roland called to his daughter. He walked over to the drapes, snatching them open to let some light into the darkened room. When he turned, he took in his daughter's disheveled appearance. She was sitting on her bed with her knees drawn to her chest wearing yesterday's clothing.

"Anastasia…what's wrong child?" Roland went to his daughter.

"Daddy," she cried. "Everything is going all wrong. I can't seem to get anything right. Why did he have to leave me, Daddy? Why?

"Baby girl, you need to let that man go. He isn't good enough for you. Don't you see that?" Roland cradled his daughter

"No! I will not divorce him! I want him to pay for walking out on me. Do you hear me, Daddy? No one walks out on me…NO ONE!"

Breaking free of his arms, Anastasia said this with renewed vigor. Wiping the tears from her face, she vowed to never cry over Justin or anyone else again. If anyone was going to hurt, it would be her wayward husband.

Chapter 22

Maalik

Maalik and Dani spent the afternoon sightseeing and shopping. Never much for shopping himself, Maalik didn't mind, as long as he was with Dani. They had slept late, exhausted from their train ordeal. While enjoying a late breakfast in a nearby restaurant, they planned out their day. Maalik told her, that because of their travel delay, his meeting had been rescheduled for the following week, freeing him up to spend his time in Toronto as he pleased.

While Dani was shoe shopping, he called to check in with his boss, to find he was on his way to North Carolina. Because of the sensitivity of the case he was working on, Maalik learned Tor would be out of commission for a few days, meaning he would be on his own. He sighed with relief. He wouldn't have to make up a story about his spending time with Dani.

Maalik looked up, at the sound of a ringing phone. Dani's phone rang for the fifth time that day. He noticed she would only glance at the screen, but would not answer it. He assumed it was the boyfriend.

"Maybe you should answer it the next time he calls," He suggested. She couldn't keep avoiding him forever.

Before she could answer him, the phone rang again. Deciding to take his advice, Dani answered.

"Devin," she answered matter-of-factly.

He didn't get to hear any more of the conversation, because she had taken the call back into the dressing room. They were in one of her favorite stores, where she was trying on clothes. Maalik waited for her to return.

He wondered what could have been so bad, to have Dani run away to another country to escape. He knew from both she and Tor that there wasn't any abuse or other parties involved, so he couldn't fathom what could have ended Dani and Devin's relationship.

"Okay, why don't we hit one more store, then go find ourselves some ridiculously expensive restaurant and have dinner? What do you say?" Dani had returned from the dressing room.

He noticed she seemed to be fine, considering she just talked to her ex. Maalik followed her out of the store, wondering what the conversation was about.

#

Devin clicked off, swiping his hand down his face. Dani didn't want him calling her again. She made it clear it was over between them and she didn't want to discuss it any further. Maybe he could have accepted that had she been in contact with Paige or Andee. Other than the note she left them, they had only received a short text, stating she was fine and would explain when she got back. No phone call, just a text.

"Well I can't let it go like that Dani," he spoke to the empty room. "I just can't let it go like that." Determined to get to the bottom of this once and for all, Devin called Tor. He had to know where she was.

#

They had just stepped out onto the sidewalk when the sky opened up into a downpour. Maalik and Dani decided to make a run for the hotel rather than call for a taxi to take them two blocks. By the time they entered the lobby, they were drenched. Shaking as much water off as they could, they hopped on the elevator to their floor, laughing at their appearance. Reaching their room, all they wanted to do was get out of their wet clothing.

Maalik handed Dani a towel to soak up the water dripping from her hair. Accepting it, she squeezed water from her long strands, as she walked towards the bathroom to change.

However, because of the soaked material, she was having trouble undoing the zipper of her dress. Maalik noticed her struggle and moved to help her. Dani pulled her wet hair to the side, giving Maalik access to the hung zipper. After a couple of tugs, he pulled the offending fastener down to the small of her back.

But instead of continuing her trek to the bathroom, Dani paused before asking him to finish what he started. She wanted him to undress her.

Hesitating for only a moment, Maalik proceeded to do just that. Slowly he pulled the straps from her shoulders and down her arms, letting the top half of her dress fall to her waist. Unhooking her strapless bra, he removed it, dropping it to the floor. Before removing more of her clothing, Maalik kissed the back of her neck as he cupped her full breasts, extracting a moan of delight from Dani.

Grasping his hands, Dani slowly moved them downward, past her flat abdomen, to the top of her panties, where Maalik took over from there. He slid his fingers inside her delicate black lace underwear, cupping her, slowly inserting his fingers inside. Dani arched her back, as he played with the bud, just above her entrance. Sensing she was about to climax, he held her tightly against him, as he moved his fingers faster, feeling her warm juices flow over them. Turning her to face him, he stripped the remainder of her clothing from her body.

Now, fully undressed, Dani stopped Maalik's hands, as he tried to remove his rain-soaked Polo shirt. She grabbed the hem of the garment, drawing it up and over his head, tossing it to the floor. She let her eyes travel from his broad chest, down to the bulge that was evident just below his belt.

Taking her time, she freed the buckle on his belt. Slowly she released the zipper and clasp, tugging the jeans from his narrow hips, letting the garment fall to the floor where he stepped out of it. Reaching inside his fly, she freed his erection from his underwear, kneading him firmly but gently. Her hands worked their magic, while he teased her mouth with his tongue.

Not wanting to wait any longer, Maalik lifted Dani and placed her on the closest bed, only leaving her for a moment to retrieve a condom. After ridding himself of his underwear, he donned the protection in record time. Once on the bed, he settled himself between her parted knees, probing intently at her unyielding opening.

Maalik placed his mouth over hers, as he pushed inside of her, swallowing her outcry. He knew he was large, so he didn't want to disturb the neighbors with his entrance. Her body quivered, as he filled her.

After Dani's body adjusted to him, Maalik moved inside of her, faster, deeper, and stronger. He enjoyed the feel of her wrapped tightly around him. Stopping for only a moment, he turned her over onto her knees. Using the headboard for balance, he drove into her repeatedly, causing the headboard to strike the wall continuously, with them both crying out at the sensations they were receiving.

Stopping once more, Maalik traded places with her. With him lying on his back, he placed her onto his massive erection, watching as she rode him. The sight of her bouncing breasts excited him even more. Maalik thought he would go crazy from the sensations he was feeling, meeting her thrust for thrust. This woman was more than he could have imagined. It was a good thing they hadn't gotten together on the train, for they would have certainly been asked to quiet down, with all the noise they were making.

Sensing Dani was about to climax again, Maalik held her in place while he thrust upward, bringing them both to completion. Sweaty and exhausted, Dani collapsed on top of him. He held her while his breathing returned to normal.

"My goodness girl, you are incredible," he said smiling. "It's a good thing it's early evening, or someone would be pounding on the wall about now," Maalik commented.

Lifting her head to look at him, she had a comment of her own. "Maalik, I have never been loved like that before in my life. You, sir, are the incredible one."

Flipping her over onto her back, Maalik quickly donned another condom.

"In that case, I think we need to get it in before our neighbors return." Kissing her briefly, Maalik drove inside of her.

Chapter 23

Evan & Jean

Alfra-Jean lay beside her sleeping husband, staring at her platinum and diamond wedding rings. She was now Mrs. Evan Bennett.

When Evan initially asked her to marry him, she thought he was joking. Yes, they had been dating for nearly a year and yes she loved him. She never thought she would marry again, especially after that fiasco with Nicolas. He led her to believe no one could love her. That was until Evan retrieved a small, black velvet box, from one of the pockets of his discarded trousers. She was in shock. This wonderful man loved her and wanted to marry her.

Still naked, Evan had gotten down on both knees as he placed the five-carat, custom-designed ring on her finger. She missed most of what he was saying because she was crying so hard. After she had gotten herself under control, she made him repeat his declaration of love for her, word for word; after which she answered a resounding yes to his proposal.

Evan had planned everything right down to the smallest detail. He made all the arrangements and reservations before he returned home that evening. The next morning they flew to St. Croix, one of his favorite vacation spots, where he owned a villa. Once they arrived, he took her shopping, to choose her dress from several he had the clerk set aside for her. After she chose the most beautiful dress imaginable, he had staff waiting at the villa to prepare her for the wedding.

When she was ready, Jean was led down to the beach, where Evan was waiting for her, along with a minister and several of the staff as attendants. Evan stood before her in a long-sleeved white cotton tunic-styled shirt with matching chinos. The hem of the pants rolled just above his ankles. Barefoot, neither required shoes on the warm sandy beach.

Jean had chosen a simple white, but elegant, sheer cotton dress, adorned with delicate lace and pearls, which was perfect for the beach ceremony. In her softly curled hair, the stylist had placed a halo of tropical flowers. Her make-up was soft, capturing her natural beauty.

Evan smiled widely when she reached him. Grasping her hands, he drew her to him. Jean looked up at her soon-to-be husband with tears of joy. She couldn't believe he had listened when she told him of her first marriage.

She had let Nicolas talk her into a tacky Vegas wedding where she spent most of her wedding night alone because he wanted to play the blackjack tables all night.

After conveying to him what a disaster her first wedding was, Evan had asked her to describe her ideal wedding, back when they first started dating. Now, here she found herself at that wedding, with him as her groom.

After the private ceremony, Evan had carried her across the sandy beach, back to the villa where the whole place had been transformed into a wonderland. There were glowing white candles of all sizes and heights, placed strategically around the open space. Among the candles, were bouquets of peach-colored flowers, from roses to rare orchids; some of Jean's favorites. To eat, Evan had chosen an assortment of local seafood, along with gourmet fruit and vegetable dishes. There were colorful displays of many desserts, including her favorite, chocolate cheesecake. Although delicious, all the food preparations were considerate of her healthy diet.

Evan had placed Jean on their wedding bed. It was decorated with a peach and white coverlet, adorned with peach and rose-colored pillows that were shaped to resemble some of the room's bouquets. He then poured them each a glass of amber heaven, from a vintage bottle of Perrier-Jouet Champagne. Handing her a crystal flute, Evan toasted his wife and Jean, her husband.

Alfra-Jean wanted to pinch herself to make sure she was not dreaming. Just in a matter of months, she had become a woman people admired. A far cry from the overweight, hateful woman, whom some of those same people had loathed. She was thankful she had come to her senses and apologized to the many people she mistreated over the years, including Evan's sister. After the last dig she made at Paige, she felt ashamed. She was grateful all was forgiven or else she would not have met such a wonderful man as her new husband.

Before Evan met Jean, he had longed to find a woman he could love and settle down with. As he sipped from his champagne, while gazing at his new wife, he felt he was truly blessed to have found her. Who would have thought he would meet his future wife at his sister's wedding?

Placing his glass on a nearby table, Evan asked his bride to dance. Taking her hand, he helped her to her feet. He pressed a button on the sound system, filling the room with music. The first song in the queue was Anthony David's *Words*. Evan listened to the lyrics. He would definitely give his wife more than the mere words he pledged in his vows. He would give her a lifetime of love and devotion.

"Are you happy Mrs. Bennett?" He asked his smiling wife. Jean pulled his mouth to hers as her answer. She was happier than any one woman had a right to be.

Sweeping her up into his arms, Evan carried her back to their bed where he lovingly placed her, as if she were the finest of China. He took his time undressing her, memorizing everything about the moment; her face radiant with her love for him, her toned and curvy body, gleaming with softness and health. He felt he was the luckiest man on earth.

After undressing her, then himself, Jean extended her hand for him to join her. Gathering her into his arms, Evan rocked her slowly, loving her with his heart as well as his body. He whispered lovingly in her ear, letting her know what he felt while making love to her as his wife, his friend, his lover. Jean wept with the love she felt for this man. A man she didn't dare dream could be hers.

Soft rain pelted the windows, as an evening storm arose, giving their wedding night the perfect rhythm, which matched the rhythm of their hearts.

#

Evan and Jean were driving to Jean's home, after their flight in from their four-day honeymoon. It was late and they were anxious to get home. They had decided to come back to Metro City to let everyone know of their marriage. They also needed to decide on what to do with her house, considering they would be living in San Francisco. They were discussing the surprise their nuptials would bring to family and friends, when one of the back tires on their car blew.

"Hold on baby," Evan told her as he wrestled with the steering wheel, trying to keep them from crashing. The car fishtailed and skidded before he was able to bring it under control. Coasting onto the shoulder to a stop, Evan unbuckled his seatbelt to attend to his startled wife.

"Baby, are you ok?" He asked her, drawing her into his arms. Jean nodded.

Kissing her cheek, Evan exited the car to inspect the damage and change the tire. Rolling up his sleeves, he noticed someone on a black motorcycle had pulled up behind them. The rider lifted the face shield on the helmet.

"Are you guys okay?" The rider was a woman. "I was about to pass you when your tire blew," she told Evan.

"Is there anything I can do to help?" She asked him concerned.

"No we're ok. I have a spare." He told her.

Evan thanked the woman and waved her off, before pulling the spare and jack from the trunk, never noticing the woman's sudden change in attitude. Once she saw them pull off the road, she too pulled onto the shoulder and hung back; driving up to offer a hand only after he exited the car. Watching Evan work, her concern turned into sudden anger. Taking one last glance, she replaced the face shield and merged back into traffic.

After he successfully swapped out the tires, Evan was about to place the damaged one in the trunk, when he noticed there was a small hole in the side wall. He assumed he had driven over some road trash that had caused the flat. Now he wasn't so sure.

He thought back to the deadly surprise they encountered in Jean's kitchen only days before. Making a mental note, he would call his sister's investigator friend Tor, when they reached Jean's. He couldn't be sure, but he thought it might be a bullet hole. Closing the trunk, Evan entered the car without mentioning his find. He did not want to frighten his wife. Vowing to get to the bottom of these seemingly random incidents, he drove them home.

☐

Chapter 24

Dani

Dani and Maalik sat in the quiet cathedral. They had spent the day exploring the city when Maalik made an offhanded remark about having kids someday. This seemed to bring sadness to Dani. He asked what was wrong when she pulled him inside the church. They had been sitting there for nearly ten minutes without saying a word when she finally spoke.

"Maalik, I did something stupid when I was younger…when I was in college." Staring straight ahead, she swallowed before she continued.

"It was my senior year and I was working down my last semester before graduation. I was so stupid," she whispered, shaking her head. Maalik didn't comment, he just waited for her to continue.

"I was having trouble with one of my history assignments and had gone to my professor for help. I was a design major. At the time, I didn't see why I needed history anyway," she added with a half-smile. "I started meeting with him whenever I had a spare moment. I was determined to get an A out of that class, even if it killed me." Finally turning to look at Maalik, she added, "And it almost did kill me too."

"His *help* sessions quickly turned into sex sessions. I was in his office one night, after hours, when he first kissed me. I didn't mind. The man was young and hot, you know? One thing led to another, and before I knew it, we were meeting in, out-of-the-way hotels every chance we got. It was all fun and games until I became pregnant. That's when everything changed."

"After I told him I was pregnant with his child, he only met with me once, and that was to give me money for an abortion. I remember, after he put the money in my hand, he told me to never contact him again. He was afraid his wife and the school would find out. He never offered to come with me. He just shoved the money at me and walked away."

"I decided to wait until after graduation to take care of it. I tried my best to act as if nothing was wrong, so

Paige, who was my roommate and best friend, wouldn't find out what a fool I'd been."

Dani stopped to look up at the mural on the ceiling as if it could clear up everything. Bringing her fingertips to her lips, she closed her eyes before she continued.

"After the graduation ceremony, my parents surprised me and my twin Dain, with a trip to Toronto. My brother and I had always talked about visiting our neighbors up north. To take in the scenery, we decided to take the train instead of flying."

"Big mistake. I hadn't planned to tell anyone about the pregnancy. I had made an appointment to see a doctor, once we got here to Toronto. I had concocted this story I would tell my twin, so I could have the procedure done without him finding out. Like I said big mistake."

She looked at the floor before continuing. "The rocking of the train made my morning sickness worse. We were pulling into the station when Dain looked at me and asked, 'You're pregnant aren't you?'. Never try to keep

anything from your twin, fraternal or not," she told him
with another half-smile.

"At that moment, I broke down and told him
everything. He wanted to fly back to find the professor and
beat him senseless. I convinced him I needed him with me,
and that it was just as much my fault as it was the
professor's."

"Anyway, Dain went with me to my appointment
and held my hand the entire time. Everything was fine until
I started hemorrhaging before I could leave the clinic. They
rushed me to the hospital where I had to undergo surgery.
As a result of that surgery, I am no longer able to have any
babies."

"I made Dain promise not to tell anyone, not even
Mom and Dad. I was too ashamed to let anyone find out
what my mistake had cost me." Dani took the hand Maalik
offered her. He gave hers a squeeze to show his support for
her hurt. She gave him a small smile before she spoke
again.

"So every time our parents would call, to see how our trip was coming along, we told them we were having a great time. Dain took such good care of me back then. I could not have asked for a better brother," she added, wiping away tears that had suddenly formed.

"By the time we had to leave for home, I was well enough to make the trip." Dani chuckled humorlessly. "I still owe my brother a trip to this lovely city.

"So you see Maalik, when Devin confided that he wanted not only me as a wife but the mother of his children…I couldn't do that to him. He deserves a whole woman. One that can give him lots of babies, not one who is damaged goods."

Maalik was about to pull her into his arms when a voice behind them spoke up.

"Baby don't you know I will love you through anything?" It was Devin.

He spotted them on the street and followed them into the church. At first, he was concerned that Dani was with this stranger until he remembered Tor had informed him, that one of his operatives was with her.

Both Dani and Maalik turned, startled. Neither of them noticed that he or anyone else had come into the church. Devin was the last person Dani expected to see.

"Devin? What are you doing here?"

Ignoring her question and Maalik, Devin came and sat down beside her, pulling her into his arms.

"Don't you know that nothing would stop me from loving you? Baby, it doesn't matter that you can't have children. I love you and want to spend the rest of my life loving you. Don't you know that?"

Dani pulled from his embrace. "You heard?" she asked him. "You heard everything?"

"Yes baby, I heard everything. Is this why you broke up with me?" She nodded. Pulling her back into his arms, Devin couldn't believe she didn't think he would understand.

"I love you no matter what," he whispered to her.

Dani locked eyes with Maalik over Devin's shoulder. When Devin moved to her side, he stood to leave. She didn't know what to say to him. She watched, as he mouthed: "it's ok, your secret is safe". She watched him turn and make his way up the aisle and out of the church.

He's a good guy and doesn't deserve this, Dani thought, as Devin spoke words of endearment.

#

Maalik made his way back to their hotel room, packing quickly. He didn't know how much time he had before Dani and her man would make their way back there. Taking a last look around, he was satisfied that he had packed all of his belongings.

He didn't want to cause her any more grief. She didn't need him anymore and he was ok with that, he told himself. If he was ok, then why did it hurt so much? Closing the door he made his way downstairs. Maalik found a cab and headed to the airport. It was time he went home.

Dani saw Maalik climb into a taxi, as she and Devin approached the hotel's entrance. She didn't get a chance to say goodbye. Although she and Devin would resolve their issues, she would always cherish the time she spent with Maalik, without regret. At the time, they were two consenting adults unattached. She didn't owe anyone an explanation for her time in Toronto, not even Devin.

Watching the cab pull away, Dani realized, that out of all the time they had spent together, she never once asked where he lived or got a phone number. And now he was lost to her forever. It seemed this city always brought pain and heartache to her life. When she left it this time, she would never return.

Chapter 25

Evan

"You were right," Tor began. "It is a bullet hole."

Evan had taken the damaged tire to Hudson Investigations where Tor had it analyzed. Evan had to wait a few days for him to return to the city, but all the while, he never let Jean out of his sight. To meet with Tor, he left her with his sister and brother-in-law. He didn't want her alone, while some maniac was on the loose.

"And you said you killed a rattlesnake in her kitchen a couple of weeks ago?" Tor asked.

Evan nodded. "When the snake showed up, I had a feeling it wasn't by accident, as the police had suggested," he informed Tor. "We had a run-in with Jean's ex a couple of days before the snake incident, now this. I'm sure he's behind all of it," Evan added.

"Look, I want you on this. I can't trust the police to get to the bottom of it."

Evan was concerned, very concerned. Someone was out to kill his wife. He wanted to know if indeed it was

Nicolas, and if so, why? Could he be this angry because she wouldn't take him back?

Although he was more than sure, Jean's former husband was involved, Evan hoped for Nicolas' sake he wasn't, or he would pay and pay dearly. No one was going to mess with his wife if he could help it. It had taken him a lifetime to find Jean, and he would be damned if some scum was going to take her away from him.

Agreeing, Tor nodded. Since Maalik had finished his last assignment, he would give him the case. He would do it himself, but he needed to follow up on his findings in North Carolina.

Chapter 26

Maalik

Maalik Wyatt sat on the side of his bed, while he listened to his friend and boss give him instructions on his next job. He swiped a hand down his face, as Tor's voice faded from him.

He was thinking about Dani Sinclair. It had been days since he left her in Toronto with Devin. However, he was still feeling the effects of losing her. He never would have guessed he would fall for someone he was given the task to keep safe. He never meant for that to happen. Maalik brought his mind back to the present when he heard Tor call his name.

"Maalik, are you still there? Arc you ok?" Tor asked.

"Yeah man, I'm fine… just fax me the particulars and I will get right on it," he told his boss.

"Hey man, did everything go alright in Toronto? Devin told me he and Dani had worked out their differences. I hoped they would. Those two belong together," Tor was saying.

Maalik begged to differ, but he couldn't tell his boss he had fallen for his client's girl; best friend or not.

"Yeah, everything went great. He showed up and I caught the first flight back home. I wish all of my cases could be that easy," he lied.

"Good. Oh, and see that you get on this right away. A woman's life may be at stake," Tor added before hanging up.

Maalik clicked off. He had to snap out of it. Dani was gone, out of his life. He had to accept that and move on. And what better way, than to jump right into the next assignment? He pushed himself off the bed and headed for the shower, while his fax machine spit out the information he would need.

"Time to get back to work and stop feeling sorry for myself," he told his reflection in the mirror.

Chapter 27

Dani

Dani sat propped against the headboard, watching Devin sleep. She had been unable to sleep since they had gotten back from Canada.

Earlier, while they made love, all she could think about was Maalik. She couldn't bring herself to let go of him. She felt bad for how things ended with them. She never meant to hurt him. Had she not believed her relationship was over with Devin, she would never have fallen into bed with him. She should have known Devin would track her down. He loved her that much.

Although she loved Devin, her mind and body kept returning to the time she spent with Maalik. She had never met a man like him. He was smart, sexy, and strong, with just the right amount of sensitivity. He was adventurous and fun, with a sense of humor she could relate to. Dani closed her eyes when she thought of their bodies colliding together. It was the most sensual joining she had ever experienced.

She looked over at Devin. She did love him and he was incredible in his own right, but there was something different and special about Maalik.

Dani sighed. She would have to let Maalik go. Besides, she wouldn't know where to start looking for him, even if she wanted to. They never exchanged contact information. It was just as well. Before they left Toronto, she had accepted Devin's proposal. Soon she would be Mrs. Devin Powers and she wasn't certain that she was happy about it.

#

Devin lay next to Dani with his eyes closed, pretending to be asleep. He waited until she left the bed before he opened them. He heard her turn on the water for a shower.

Devin was concerned. He knew something was off, something was wrong. Although they had resolved their problems, she was still restless. She seemed conflicted. He noticed she hadn't been sleeping well since they returned from Toronto. He wondered if the man he found her with had something to do with her mood. Maalik was his name.

When he spotted them together on the street that day, before they entered the church, he thought he recognized a familiarity between the two. When he asked Dani about it, she denied knowing Maalik before her trip. Stating that she had met him on the train and had run into him again, while she was in the city.

Devin knew Maalik worked for Tor and what his purpose was for being there. Dani, however, had no idea who he was. But still, they seemed as if they were the best of friends, almost as if they were lovers. Devin sat up shaking his head. They couldn't have slept together. Could they?

He quickly pushed that thought from his mind. Tor was an upstanding guy and he was certain his employees were beyond reproach. Devin refused to believe anything had taken place between the two. He decided Dani just clung to the man because he was a familiar face in an unfamiliar city.

"Yes, that has to be it," he whispered to himself.

Besides, she accepted his proposal of marriage. Something he had wanted from the very beginning, from the first moment he saw her. He loved her and she loved him.

Raking his fingers through his disheveled hair, Devin got up to join Dani in the shower.

☐

Chapter 28

Nicolas

Nicolas sat alone in his apartment staring at the blackened TV screen. He had turned it off and threw the remote across the room. He couldn't believe the mess he had gotten himself into. All this because he decided to play the ponies.

Sighing deeply, he got up to get a beer from the refrigerator. He had been looking forward to spending some time with Lucinda, but she called to say she had to work tonight. One of the girls and gotten sick, so she had to fill in for her. She had been doing that a lot lately. He wondered if she was telling the truth.

Lucinda liked money and lots of it. Although she was pulling down a good chunk of change, working the pole with her routine, along with her private acts, she still wanted more. Because of her love of money, Nicolas believed she may have dumped him for deeper pockets.

Money, everything came back to the money. Nicolas had made a deal with Fye Freddy to get himself off the hook, but he was having second thoughts. Shaking his head, he knew he didn't have a choice. Jean may not be one of his favorite people, but he didn't know if he could live with her death. It was either him or Jean, so it was the best deal he could have made.

Nicolas decided he didn't want that beer after all. Placing it back inside the refrigerator, he decided to drive out to his ex-wife's instead, to take a look around. He made the right choice and he was sticking to it. Besides, he didn't owe the bitch anything. Especially since she wouldn't take him back.

He had grabbed his keys when his phone rang. Hoping it was Lucinda with a change of heart, he smiled, only to be disappointed by the caller. Glancing at the display, it was his tormentor, Freddy. Nicolas started to let it go to voice mail but thought better of it. Freddy would only send his thugs to rough him up again, and he certainly didn't want that.

Sighing, he answered.

Chapter 29

Fye Freddy

Fye Freddy hung up the phone from his second call of the night. He was angry, but controlled. Things were not going the way he had hoped. At least one of his special projects should have been finished by now, but fate didn't seem to be on his side. He needed it done before his benefactor became antsy. His second project, although personal, should have been completed also.

Fredrick Armand Davis, aka Fye Freddy, never thought getting his money back from Nicolas would be this difficult. After persuading him to sign on the dotted line, he thought the rest of it would be a piece of cake. A job that should have taken a few minutes seemed to be taking an eternity.

Grinding his teeth, Freddy reached for one of his expensive hand-rolled cigars, while he thought over his dilemma. It wasn't as if he needed the money, considering what he was getting paid to complete his other project, but it was the principle of the thing. Freddy had earned his reputation by being ruthless and he planned to keep it that way.

Back in the day, when he was a small-time thug selling weed in an alley, he had earned the name Fye Freddy, because he was known to have the best product; the fire, or the *Fye*, as it was known in the hood.

As he moved through the ranks of organized crime, the name stuck with him. Freddy liked it because it brought him a certain level of respect. Especially when he became his own boss, with the help of some very influential people. People who fronted him money to open his chain of strip clubs to add to his other less desirable businesses.

Freddy, after lighting his cigar, had an idea. Although he decided, that getting his money back from Nicolas shouldn't be his top priority at the moment, he saw a way to light a fire under both jobs. Picking up the phone again, he dialed the number back.

"I know you have your hands full, so let's get that other job out of the way as soon as possible. You can get back to my debt collection later. But listen…if by you chance find a way to get both done just as quickly, I will pay you double." Satisfied he would now be able to clear both projects, because of the pay boost, Freddy hung up; pleased with himself. The quicker he could get things done, the more avenues he could pursue, which meant the more money he could spend.

#

The woman smiled as she closed her phone with a snap. Although the work proved more difficult than first thought, it was quickly becoming more lucrative. After pulling on her gloves, she placed her helmet over her head. It was time to get down to business. She would have to use some different tactics if she was to be successful. She felt, in one aspect, Nicolas Hampton was the key. He held the answers she needed.

Kickstarting the bike; she rode off into the night, only to be followed by a black pickup.

Chapter 30

Hannah

Hannah opened her door to the most amazing bouquet of perfect flowers she had ever seen. She was just about to reach for her purse to give the delivery guy a tip when Jayden's handsome face appeared around the arrangement.

"You don't have to tip me. Your beautiful smile is all the thanks I need," he told a surprised Hannah.

"Get in here," she told him grinning. She stepped aside, allowing Jayden entrance into her home.

"Jayden, they're lovely, thank you." Hannah smiled at the beautiful gesture.

He looked around for a spot to place them. "Where do you want these?" He watched Hannah, while she moved some books from a trunk that doubled as a coffee table.

"Here, you can put them here." Hannah was surprised but happy to see him. They had been out on several dates, since their first outing, but for her, it wasn't nearly enough. So opening the door to Jayden was a welcomed treat.

"I hope you don't mind me dropping by. I happened to be in your neighborhood, and as I drove past this florist...well, I had to get them. They seem to have your name on them."

"I'm glad you came by. Won't you have a seat?" She gestured towards the sofa.

Instead of accepting the proffered seat, Jayden gathered her into his arms, kissing her as if he would stop breathing if he couldn't. Drawing her closer, he deepened the kiss, tasting her with his probing tongue. He had been thinking about her all day. Finally coming up for air, he drew his thumb across her kiss-swollen lips.

"So I guess that means you missed me, huh?" Hannah asked, still reeling from his welcomed assault on her senses.

"Maybe I should go," Jayden whispered, suddenly feeling awkward. He didn't know what had come over him, but he just felt the need to kiss her. The previous times he was in her presence, he would always peck her on the cheek. But seeing her today, he wanted more than just a chaste kiss. He wanted to taste her lips.

Making a move to leave, Jayden suddenly found himself being pulled back. This time, Hannah kissed him, relaying what she was feeling for him. Still unsure as to what was actually happening between them, Jayden gently pulled away.

Reading the uncertainty in his eyes, Hannah realized she would have to make things plain for him. She knew he was taking things slowly, because of past hurts in both their lives, but for her, the time for slow had passed, and she needed him to understand that.

Hannah breathlessly answered his unspoken question. "Yes Jayden, I want you. So don't analyze it, just do it."

Doing what he was told, Jayden pushed his doubt away and lifted Hannah off her feet. With her arms wrapped around his neck, and his around her waist, he carried her to her bedroom. Placing her on her feet again, he didn't think or analyze.

"I hope this isn't one of your favorites," he told her, just before ripping her blouse from her body. Hannah's answer was a satisfied grin.

Not needing any more prompting, Jayden quickly stripped her of the remainder of her clothing. Undressing himself just as quickly, he retrieved a condom from his wallet, before joining her on the bed.

Hannah watched him roll the condom over his generous erection. They both were breathing heavily by the time he finished the task, with both anticipating what would come next. She continued to watch, as he positioned himself between her thighs.

Placing her long shapely legs over his shoulders, and pulling her towards him, Jayden plunged inside her, extracting a cry of pleasure from Hannah. He rode her. Savoring every expression that played across her face. He couldn't believe the sensations he was receiving, by being inside of this gorgeous woman.

Jayden planted his mouth over hers, with his tongue plunging deep inside, while he continued his sensual assault on her body, on her soul. Picking up the tempo, he rotated his hips, venturing deeper within her.

Hannah climaxed multiple times, nearly with each stroke of his penis. She had never had a sexual awakening, like the one she was experiencing with Jayden.

Just as Hannah thought her body couldn't handle anymore, Jayden stopped for only a moment, before turning her over and placing her flat onto her stomach. Spreading her legs wide, he lay on top of her. He grasped her outstretched hands, hands that were tightly clutching the sheets, before he entered her again.

This time, his thrusts were slow, but ever so deep. Each thrust seemingly vibrated from his body into hers. Jayden was in paradise. He felt her come again and again, exciting him more than he could imagine. Not able to hold off any longer, he thrust one final time, timing her last climax with his own, bringing them both to completion.

Breathing heavily, Jayden rolled off of Hannah and pulled her against him. That was the most intense encounter he'd had. He glanced down at a satisfied Hannah, who was trying to catch her breath.

"I hope that's what you meant when you told me not to analyze," he told her between breaths. This woman is incredible, he thought.

Having gathered herself, Hannah responded. "Yes, it was. I wanted you without you having to think the act through. I've noticed you tend to overanalyze things. I know it's probably due to your job, but Mr. Fireman, with this flame, you can always take whatever means necessary to put it out," Hannah reassured him with a grin. And to emphasize her point, she placed his hand between her thighs.

Taking it as an invitation, Jayden donned more protection, before extinguishing another fire that was blazing wildly inside of her.

☐

Chapter 31

Justin

Justin Graham was not used to being the one under surveillance, but both Tor and KT thought it was necessary. They were still unsure as to who was trying to kill him, but all were convinced that his wife was behind it. No one else had a motive. The problem was proving it. It had been a while since the brake incident, but everyone was in agreement, that the person or persons involved would most likely try again.

"I am very capable of protecting myself, you know." Justin expressed this to KT the moment she let herself into his house. She had gone out to pick up a few things she needed to prepare their dinner. Since Justin's accident, she had been his shadow. Following him into the office, meetings, wherever he went.

"Yes I know you are a top-notch investigator, but it's been a while since you've been out in the field. Your instincts may not be as sharp as they used to be, not to mention you're working with one arm," KT informed him.

She had listened to his gripes over being babysat since the accident. And to add to his frustration, his arm was in a cast.

"Ouch," Justin replied. "You don't hold back do you?"

"Why should I? It's the truth. When you aren't in the field day-to-day, you tend to become relaxed; not watching your back, which can lead to someone getting the jump on you. When was the last time you worked a case yourself?" She asked him, curious.

"It's been a while," Justin mumbled, while not meeting her eyes.

She was right. Even though he wouldn't admit to the length of time, she could take a guess that it had been years, since he'd worked a serious case. Sitting behind a desk every day, delegating work, he had become soft whether he realized it or not. It didn't take survival skills to coordinate and delegate. While he personally managed cyber issues for some of his clients, it wasn't the same as being out there on the streets, running surveillance, or chasing after bad guys.

Pleased she'd made her point, KT continued into the kitchen. Aside from her investigative abilities, she was an excellent cook. Since she had to stay with Justin, she insisted that she do all the cooking. All Justin wanted was takeout or to eat out at restaurants, which she didn't think was a good idea until after the culprit was apprehended.

Following her into the kitchen, Justin decided to ignore her assessment of his current lack of abilities. "So what's on the menu tonight," Justin asked, genuinely curious. Although he wouldn't admit it, he enjoyed watching her cook, and the food wasn't half bad either.

"I thought we would have my special meatloaf with baked sweet potatoes and a fresh green salad that will consist of mixed greens, apples, honey-roasted pecans, and dried cranberries. And to top of the salad, a pomegranate dressing.

"And for dessert?" He asked. Justin fantasized that she would breathlessly tell him, she was for dessert.

The moment KT arrived at his home, Justin observed her. Finding her more than attractive, he often found himself wondering what she would be like in bed.

"For dessert, we will be having a raspberry sorbet," she answered, not realizing she had disappointed him with her answer.

Justin mentally shrugged, bringing his attention back to their meal. "So what makes the meatloaf special?" He asked. He didn't think anything special could be done with meatloaf.

"What makes my meatloaf special are the carrots," she informed him." Rolling her eyes, at his puzzled expression, she explained. She fully expected him to turn up his nose at the mention of carrots in the loaf.

"I add shredded carrots to my meatloaf, along with some other special ingredients. And before you ask about the other ingredients, if I told you, I would have to kill you," she deadpanned. A second passed before they both burst into laughter.

Still smiling, Justin commented on her laughter. "You know, I didn't think you could smile, let alone laugh. It looks good on you. You should do it more often," he suggested.

Since his ordeal began, he hadn't gotten anything but business from KT. She never smiled or joked. This was the first time. He hoped maybe she was taking a liking to him since she didn't seem to like anything or anyone.

KT wiped the smile from her face. "Why don't you choose a wine to go with dinner," she said, dismissing him.

Justin sighed, as he left the kitchen, to retrieve a bottle from the collection in the huge custom pantry. He was disappointed. He was sure they had made a break though in their otherwise detached relationship. But in the blink of an eye, the moment was gone. And if he read her correctly, that lightheartedness wouldn't return ever again.

#

"I must admit, when you said you added carrots to the meatloaf, I was a bit skeptical," Justin told her, "but this has got to be the best meatloaf I have ever eaten." Placing his fork on his empty plate, Justin leaned back into his chair. He had thoroughly enjoyed the meal, so much so, he had a second helping.

KT took a swallow from her wine glass before she answered him. "I am glad you enjoyed it. It's one of my favorite meals."

"Are you always so health conscience?" He asked. Since she had been there, all the meals she prepared were healthy. When she cooked the first meal, after telling him what was in it, he had frowned, convinced it would be tasteless. But to his surprise, it was delicious, as were all of her dishes.

"You are what you eat," she told him.

Rising from the table, she prepared to do her sweep of the outside perimeter of the house, while he gathered the dishes. They had worked out the routine from the beginning. Even though he had a broken arm, Justin insisted, if she cooked, he would do the dishes while she checked on things outside. She had agreed, provided he used the dishwasher, otherwise, she could just see him breaking more dishes than he cleaned.

KT picked up her Glock G17 from the coffee table, before making her way outside. Locking the door behind her, she turned to scan the street. She thought about Justin, as she made her way around to the back of the house. He was beginning to get under her skin. They had spent a few nights together under the same roof, with her often thinking about what he was like as a man, and not her boss.

Although their rooms were on opposite ends of the house, she would often make her rounds to his bedroom, while he slept. The night before, unable to sleep, she decided to get herself a glass of water. But before she could enter the kitchen, she heard him rummaging around in the refrigerator for his nightly snack. Not wanting to make her presence known, KT hid in the shadows watching him.

From the looks of his wet hair, Justin had just stepped out of the shower. This was not what caught KT's attention. What grabbed her attention was the fact that he was completely nude. She watched him pull the leftovers from the refrigerator with his one good hand. She noticed how his muscles rippled, as he reached for a plate from the top shelf of the cupboard. Although she could only see the backside of him, she imagined what the front of him looked like.

Coming to her senses and grasping this was inappropriate, she made her way back to her room, a little shaken. It had been years since she had been in a relationship. After leaving the military, she concentrated on what to do with her life next. She hadn't time for relations and her body had intimately reminded her of that fact.

When she made it back to her bedroom, KT shook her head, at her moment of weakness. Pressing her back against the closed door, she tried willing her body to behave. She knew she had to stay on task and keep her head in the game. If she didn't, it could very well cost her everything.

Noting that everything was calm outside, KT made her way back inside the house. She lowered the lights in the living room as if it were her routine. She never left the area pitch dark, in case she needed to make her way through the house quickly. Checking the doors and windows once more, she made her way back to her room. She checked to make sure she had bottled water. She didn't want to be tempted to spy on Justin again tonight.

#

It was late when Justin made his way from the kitchen with his nightly snack. Just as he entered the dimly lit room, he heard noises just outside the patio doors that led out into a side yard. Quietly placing his loaded plate on a nearby table, he slipped into a pair of gray sweatpants that hung haphazardly over the back of a chair. He listened for the sound again, as he grabbed his handgun from the top of a bureau.

Easing his way to the sliding door, he peered through the blinds. Not seeing anything, he cautiously opened the door and stepped outside onto the tiled patio, only to be met with gunfire. Retreating quickly behind a retaining wall, Justin returned fire.

While he waited for the intruder to fire again, he chanced a look, to find a dark figure running across the yard. Before he could make out who it was, the figure was gone. Carefully pushing himself up from the ground, Justin ran in the direction of the retreating intruder, only to collide with KT walking back to the house.

"Did you see who it was?" He asked her.

KT shook her head. "Too dark...they disappeared into the woods before I could get a good look," she told him. "Come on, let's get back to the house."

She followed Justin back to the patio. Taking one final look around her, KT stepped through the door, locking it behind her. She was angry she was unable to do her job effectively.

Placing his gun on the bed, Justin sighed. "Now that somebody has thrown gunplay into the mix, we have to get the police involved," he informed her. She reluctantly nodded her agreement.

While Justin phoned the police, KT surmised that her job had just become more difficult.

#

Detective Eric Valero watched the pacing young woman with interest. She seemed to be agitated and he wanted to know why.

He had been called to the scene of a shooting at his friend Justin Graham's home. Justin called him immediately after reporting the incident to the nearby precinct. Justin's business interactions with the police department had netted him quite a few allies on the force, including Valero.

Eric Valero was of African and Hispanic descent. His mother was from Puerto Rico and his father, a native of Detroit, had been killed on the job before he was born; and before he could marry his mother.

Inheriting features from both worlds, he always attracted unwavering attention from women. Although he wasn't a fan of that kind of blatant interest, it puzzled him that KT Ellis had barely glanced at him.

Eric nodded in her direction. "What's with her?"

Justin glanced at an agitated KT. "She's frustrated at not being able to catch this guy," Justin told him. "From what I gather, she's a perfectionist, and the perpetrator getting away from her tonight, does not sit too well with Ms. Ellis."

Nodding his understanding, Eric looked over his notes, as he finished his interview with his friend.

"I think it's about time I got Ms. Ellis' take on the night's events," he told Justin.

"Good luck with that," he remarked with a chuckle. He could see from the expression on KT's face, it was not going to be an easy task.

As he made his way across the room, Eric visually took the woman in. She appeared to be a little rough around the edges, but a beauty nonetheless. Her stance told him he would likely have to proceed with caution.

"Ms. Ellis, I'm Detective Eric Valero—"

"KT," she gruffly interrupted him.

"Okay, KT it is," he agreed with a rise of an eyebrow. "Can you give me your version of what happened tonight?"

While carefully considering her answer, before she spoke, KT finally gave Eric Valero some attention. She was so caught up in not accomplishing her mission, that she was barely aware the police had arrived.

After giving the handsome detective a once over, she found Eric Valero worthy of more than a quick examination. Unlike her usual perusals, she discreetly gave him a full inspection but still managed to remain indifferent. She took in his height, as well as his wonderfully built body, along with his obvious Hispanic ancestry. With his wavy black hair and olive-toned skin, he was indeed worthy of several glances. Making sure her face did not reflect what her mind and body had registered, KT answered the detective's questions.

"I was about to prepare for bed when I heard gunfire coming from the east side of the house. I grabbed my gun and ran outside towards that end of the house. Once

I got there, I saw a figure fleeing the yard. I gave chase until I lost them in the woods behind the house," she told the detective.

Eric listened, while KT gave him the rundown of the night's events. He asked her why neither she nor Justin bothered to report their earlier suspicions about the failed brakes, which caused Justin's accident.

"Mr. Graham preferred to keep this in-house if he could," she explained. "But after tonight's shooting, he didn't have a choice. He had to get the police involved," KT added.

Satisfied with her answers, Eric had just one more question to ask her. "How did you come to be employed by Justin." He knew all of Justin's employees and all of them were men.

"Actually, I am employed by Hudson Investigations. As part of my contract with Tor Hudson, I am to be available for assignments with Graham Inc," she clarified.

"Were you hired before or after Justin suspected his wife?"

"Before," she answered. KT was accustomed to answering only the questions asked, nothing more.

Feeling she would only parrot more of what Justin had already given him, Eric felt he had enough information, for now.

Tapping his pad with his pen, he wondered if Justin and KT had more than a working relationship. She was living in his home, although it was supposedly to keep him safe. He wondered if anything other than business had transpired between them. He would have to ask Justin.

"Okay, KT. I think I have all that I need. Will you be staying here tonight?" He asked her this more out of curiosity than professional need.

"Yes. I will be here until this case is solved," she told the detective. *Hmm. Is that a note of interest I hear in his voice?* KT wondered.

Without thinking she spoke again; hoping she was reading him correctly, she quickly added an answer to the question she knew he really wanted to ask. "Oh, and detective…it's strictly business between Mr. Graham and I."

Eric nodded, as he turned to make a few more notes. "That's good to know," he answered, under his breath, before heading for the door. He was relieved. Although he valued Justin's friendship, he wanted the woman more.

Chapter 32

Evan

Evan looked out the window, at the rain that had begun to fall. He and Jean had finished dinner and were about to enjoy a cozy night together. While he enjoyed the rain's rhythmic tapping on the pane, his thoughts wandered to the attempts on Jean's life. Even though what he and Tor believed was a bullet hole in the tire, he wasn't quite ready to go to the police yet. And it didn't help that the first incident was labeled an accident by the responding officers. What he wanted, was to put his hands on Nicolas himself, *before* the police were involved.

He still hadn't told his wife about the tire or his visit with Tor Hudson. He didn't think it was necessary to include her in this mess until it was solved. Jean still believed the snake incident was an accident, and he continued to let her believe it. He loved her and wanted to spare her as much hurt as possible.

After his visit with Tor, he had driven back to this sister's more concerned than ever. Anderson, his sister's husband, met him in the yard when he arrived. He wanted to know what was going on. Apparently, Jean had filled them in on finding the snake in the kitchen. Anderson felt there had to be more to the story. Especially after Evan pulled him aside; asking him to keep an eye on Jean while he was gone.

Evan reluctantly explained to Anderson, his and Tor's suspicions about the strange incidents, and who they thought may be behind it all. Knowing how Anderson felt about keeping secrets from his wife, Evan made it clear he would not be informing Jean until the issue was resolved. He did not want her frightened. Anderson agreed to explain the circumstances to Paige.

Touching his fingertips to the rain-cooled glass, Evan smiled when he remembered his sister's face when they announced their marriage. She was surprised but happy for them both. With their difficulties in the past, she and Jean had become good friends; now they were family.

Thinking of his wife, Evan wondered what was keeping her. She had gone into the kitchen to mix one of her special smoothies for dessert. He chuckled at her seriousness to maintain her weight. Personally, he didn't think she needed to work so hard.

"Jean baby, are you coming in soon? I'm about to queue the movie." Evan called out to her, but got no answer.

Quickly, dread drained his face of color, when he remembered the last time something happened in the kitchen. Evan dropped the remote control he was holding, before sprinting for the kitchen. He found his wife on her knees, gasping for air, unable to speak.

Grabbing her instantly, Evan nearly panicked, as he watched her lips turn blue. Reaching for the cordless phone on the counter, he dialed 911, giving the dispatcher the necessary information.

Evan tried everything he could think of to help Jean to breathe, but his mind had drawn a blank in his distress. Fear gripped him, as Jean slowly closed her eyes, just as paramedics arrived. He watched in horror, when she stopped breathing, requiring them to give her CPR. He was shaking, by the time they got her to breathe again. After Jean was stabilized enough to be transported, he called Anderson and Tor to meet them at the hospital.

#

"Evan, Evan…what happened?" Paige called out to her brother, as she waddled towards him. Paige was eight months pregnant with her first child. She arrived with her husband, along with Tor and Andee, Tor's wife.

Evan had been nervously pacing the length of the waiting room, with renewed fear. Once they arrived in the ED, he was directed to the waiting area for updates. Since they arrived, the only update he received was the medical team was still working to save his wife.

"I…I don't know. We were about to watch a movie and…" Evan grabbed his sister, hugging her tight. He couldn't believe he nearly lost his wife, and could still lose her if they couldn't determine what was wrong. Tears were streaming down the siblings' faces; neither was able to speak.

"Mr. Bennett?" The doctor asked, entering the room.

"Yes, yes... I am Evan Bennett," Evan answered while wiping the tears from his face. "How is she...can I see her?" Still racked with emotion, he was barely able to get the words out.

"Mr. Bennett, your wife had a close call tonight. It seems she ingested a fair amount of peanuts. Are you aware of her allergy to nuts?" The doctor asked.

Nodding, Evan was confused. "Yes... I am, but how is that possible? There isn't a nut to be found in our house. We're careful of bringing anything into the house without reading the label first."

Evan was perplexed. How could this happen? Had he known it was an allergic reaction he would have used an EpiPen to help his wife. However, because their home was a hazard-free zone, it never crossed his mind her attack could be an allergic reaction.

"Well, our tests show that was the cause of your wife's trauma. I suggest you throw out any and everything you even remotely think may have caused this. Oh…and yes, you may see her. She's asking for you. We've moved her upstairs for overnight observation. She's in room 302." Nodding to the others, the doctor left.

"I don't understand. How could that have happened?" Evan was more upset than ever.

"Evan tell me. What was Jean doing just before she collapsed?" Tor asked him.

Sighing, Evan closed his eyes and searched his mind. "She was in the kitchen making one of her shakes. She usually has one after dinner. It's a part of her meal plan," he told him.

"What's in it…do you know?" Tor pressed for more.

"Some fruit, milk, and some sort of protein powder that she…," Suddenly Evan's eyes widened with a thought. "Do you think it was in the powder?"

"We'll see," Tor told him. "Give me your keys. I'll check it out."

"I am coming with you," Anderson told him. Evan gave them the keys to their home. Anderson and Tor kissed their wives and left.

"I need to see my wife," Evan told Paige and Andee after Tor and Anderson left.

"Go…go, we'll be along in a little while. Go take care of Jean." Paige hugged her brother before he raced off to the elevator.

"Paige, what the hell is going on?" Andee asked her friend. "Tor said something about someone trying to kill Jean?"

Paige nodded. "It seems Jean's ex-husband showed up at her house a few weeks ago, before she and Evan got married. The man was trying to get her to take him back. Unfortunately for him, Evan was there and he threw the bum out. Evan thinks he's trying to get even with her for not taking him back."

"So this is how Tor became involved?" Andee asked. Paige nodded.

Andee didn't ask many questions about her husband's business, because most of his work was confidential. But these were her friends and she was concerned.

"What a horrible mess," Andee added shaking her head.

#

"Did you find it?" Tor asked Anderson. They were in the Bennett's kitchen, tearing it apart, hoping to at least find the protein powder.

When they first arrived, they found the kitchen, as they assumed Evan and the paramedics had left it. But when they started looking around, they weren't so sure. They found some of the fruit Jean used, sitting on a cutting board. The milk was on the counter also. But what was puzzling, was the blender, the glass Jean drank from, and the protein powder were all gone.

"I guess we can safely say the bastard came back and cleaned up behind himself," Anderson ventured.

"Dammit! Anderson man, I'm slippin'! I should have come straight here, instead of going to the hospital." Tor was beside himself. Had he arrived earlier, he may have caught the culprit in the act of removing the evidence.

"Hey man, don't take it too hard. Who would have thought the son of a bitch would have had the balls to come back here so soon?" Anderson shook his head. "And besides, you didn't have all the information at the time." Anderson felt Tor's pain. Whoever was out to get Jean meant business, and they meant not to get caught doing it.

☐

Chapter 33

A few days later

Paige hugged Jean when she and Evan arrived for the party. "I am so glad you're feeling better," Paige told her.

Evan and Jean had come to the Stone's for a belated wedding celebration, which Paige and Anderson were hosting. All of their friends and family were invited to wish the happy couple well.

"That makes three of us," Jean said. "That was quite a scare, and your brother has been watching me like a hawk. I can't seem to go anywhere without him tagging along," she joked with an adoring grin at Evan.

Paige glanced up at her brother. He still hadn't told Jean his suspicions about who was trying to hurt her. Reading her concern, Evan shook his head slightly; indicating they would discuss the matter later.

"Well, I'm just glad you're here. I was going to postpone the party, but Evan informed me you were going stir-crazy being cooped up inside. Look, come on in and join the festivities. Everyone is out back on the patio," she told them.

Everyone included Tor and Andee who were the first to arrive. Tor wanted to get there before the other guests, to check out the neighborhood. He didn't want any surprises. He was way ahead of Evan before he called with his concerns. Unbeknownst to anyone, besides Tor, he had help. Maalik Wyatt was parked across the street watching the house. Tor felt he had everything covered, to ensure the newlyweds a safe and joyous celebration.

#

Maalik sat in his truck watching the guests arrive at the Stones. He had discreetly shadowed the Bennetts from their house, to make sure they weren't being followed. After backing into the driveway of the vacant house across the street, Maalik texted Tor to inform him he was in place. With the backdrop of the heavily treed yard, his black truck blended into the darkness; invisible to anyone looking in that direction.

Maalik took pictures of every vehicle and person who parked along the street. Most of those parking, made their way up the walk to the Stone's, who granted them entrance soon after they rang the doorbell. There were only a few, who visited the surrounding neighbors.

When there was a lull in activity, Maalik looked over his case notes. He still didn't know what to make of the woman on the motorcycle, he encountered, during his surveillance of the Bennett's house. He wondered how many females rode that same bike. Although he never got a good look at her, he didn't like where his mind was taking him, as to the woman's identity. He only saw her without her helmet once, and that was when she stopped to receive a phone call. Unfortunately for him, the street was dark and she had her back to him.

He followed the woman to the home of a well-known gangster in town, Fye Freddy. Tor had gotten a lead on Freddy when he'd gone back east on another job. It seemed Freddy was a busy boy.

After Tor had given him the assignment, he set up surveillance outside of Jean Bennett's house. While he was there the first night, the woman on the motorcycle had shown up, just cruising the neighborhood. But when she came a second time, he followed her back to Fye Freddy's, where she stayed for the rest of the night.

Maalik had been sitting in front of Freddy's house the night Jean was poisoned. After spotting Nicolas driving through his former wife's neighborhood, he decided to follow him—right to Fye Freddy's. He was more certain than ever that Nicolas was involved in the attempts on Jean Bennett's life. He just couldn't prove it. And how was he linked to Freddy? Anytime someone was involved with Fye Freddy, it was never good. But after Jean's poisoning, and with him having eyes on Nicholas, he wasn't so sure of his direct involvement and he shared this with Tor. There was no way Nicholas could be in two places at the same time, which brought him back to the mystery woman. How did she fit into this?

So here he sat outside Anderson Stone's house, to see if Nicolas or the mystery woman would show up there.

After a while, a car pulled into the Stone's driveway, instead of parking on the street as the other guests had. The occupants didn't immediately exit the car. Although he didn't think the individual, after Jean, would be that bold to park in the driveway, the move piqued Mallik's interest. Leaning forward, he held his night vision camera to his eye.

Looking through the viewfinder, he watched the two occupants converse. Finally exiting the car, Maalik quickly concluded, from the man's resemblance, that this was Anderson's brother with his date. Snapping the couple's photo anyway, he watched them until they entered the Stone's home.

#

"Are you sure you're ready for this?" Hannah asked Jayden.

They had arrived at his brother's house to celebrate Evan and Jean's marriage. He knew everyone would be there, including Andee and her new husband. He was still a little uncertain, but he was glad he asked Hannah to join him.

When the invitation arrived in the mail, he had no intentions of going to the gathering. He didn't think he was ready to face Andee and Tor. But after mentioning it to Hannah, she convinced him to attend; citing he couldn't keep avoiding his ex and her husband forever. Not to mention, if he continued to do so, he would miss spending time with his brother. Anderson was due to be a father soon and he wanted to be a part of his niece or nephew's life.

Hannah was right. Andee was married and there wasn't a thing he could do about it. It was high time he moved on. And what better person to do that with, than the woman sitting beside him?

Jayden had been quiet on the short flight in. He wondered how he would feel seeing Andee after all this time. Will it hurt or will he feel nothing? There was only one way to find out. Besides, since he and Hannah had become close, the pain of losing Andee had lessened.

Hannah had introduced him to a whole new concept of life after Andee.

He had never had a woman to encourage him to live life without having to map it out first. For most of his life, Jayden had set boundaries and made plans. Plans he usually followed to the letter. But seeing life through Hannah's eyes, he concluded his way of life was much too structured and usually left little room for error. This made his life somewhat predictable and yes, boring. Those ridged boundaries were the cause of him losing Andee in the first place.

Pulling Hannah to him, Jayden kissed her. "Let's do this.

Exiting the car, Jayden walked around to the passenger side to assist Hannah. Holding hands, they made their way to the door. After ringing the bell, Jayden smiled at Hannah, while they waited for someone to answer. They didn't have to wait long before Anderson greeted them.

"Hey little brother, come on in." Anderson, glad to see his brother, grabbed him in a brotherly bear hug. They hadn't seen much of each other, since he broke things off with Andee.

"And who do we have here?" He asked of Hannah, after releasing Jayden.

"Hannah, I would like you to meet my big brother Anderson. And Anderson, this is my lady Hannah Pierce." Jayden was all smiles introducing Hannah to his brother. He felt pride in this. Emotionally, he had come a long way.

"Oh, and this is my very pregnant sister-in-law Paige, Anderson's wife." Paige had joined her husband at the door. "Paige this is Hannah."

Hannah had extended her hand for a shake, only to be pulled into an embrace by Paige.

"Hannah, no handshakes here. A friend of Jayden's is considered family," she informed her. "Come on in and meet everyone." Pulling her way from Jayden, Paige winked at her husband.

After Paige led Hannah deeper into the house, to meet some of the other guests, Anderson turned to his brother.

"Lovely girl, where did you meet her?" He was glad Jayden had found someone and wasn't alone. He knew how hard it hit him after losing Andee.

Jayden chuckled. "Well actually, I first met Hannah in the airport at home. This was right after I had found out about Andee. I literally knocked her down." Jayden's smile widened, as he told his brother the tale of how he and Hannah met.

"So she turned out to be the reporter who interviewed you?"

Jayden nodded. "And the rest, I guess you can say is history."

"Hey bro, not to change the subject or anything…but are you going to be okay with Tor and Andee? They are here you know," Anderson warned him.

"You know Anderson, surprisingly yes. And it's all due to that feisty woman I brought with me." Jayden assured his brother he was fine with them being there. He was surprised himself, at the peace he felt.

"Well if that's the case, let's go join the party."
Anderson led the way.

#

Maalik placed his notes aside and was just about to
take a sip from his coffee cup when a bronze Range Rover
pulled up and parked near his driveway. He watched the
man exit the car and then walked around to the passenger
side. When he opened the door and the woman stepped out,
Maalik's heart raced. It was Dani. Quickly raising his
camera, he took rapid photos of her and Devin.

He watched them cross the street and make their
way up the walk to the house. Maalik's heart beat faster,
when Dani turned, seemingly to look in his direction. He
raised the camera again, only to look directly into her eyes
for a quick second. Although he knew she couldn't see him,
he reasoned she somehow sensed him.

Maalik immediately wished he could have
something stronger than coffee.

#

Dani turned to look into the yard across the street. She had the strangest feeling they were being watched. Not seeing anything, she turned towards the door when Paige opened it. Glancing at the yard once more, she entered the house.

#

"Well, I see you guys finally made it," Dain remarked, kissing his sister's cheek. "And I don't mean to the party." He, and his fiancé Taylor, had arrived minutes before Dani and Devin.

Dain had been concerned about his sister since she told him she was taking some time away to be alone. He wanted to know what was going on with her. She never wanted to be alone, unless there was a problem she needed to sort through. Although she was reluctant to tell him at first, she explained what transpired between her and Devin, after his and Taylor's engagement party. Understanding, Dain promised her he wouldn't divulge her whereabouts.

"And Devin, I hope there aren't any hard feelings between us. She's my sister, and if she tells me to stay quiet then…" Dain trailed off with a shrug.

"No need to explain man. I understand," Devin assured him. He knew Dain was only protecting his sister.

"Hey Dani, Devin. How are things going? This was Taylor, Dain's fiancée. "And congratulations you guys on your engagement." Taylor beamed; happy for the couple.

Hugging Taylor, Dani plastered on a smile and responded. "Everything's great," she smoothly lied. "And thank you."

Nothing had been right in her world since she left Toronto. She still felt guilty for leaving things unfinished with Maalik. And to top it off, she couldn't get him out of her head. Each time she and Devin made love, she wanted it to be Maalik inside of her, not Devin.

"You guys, the party is out back," Paige called to them. "You have to come see my brother and Jean dance. She is doing just fine, but Evan never could keep a rhythm," she laughed. "Oh, and Taylor, your brother and

Mia are putting everyone to shame. Those two know how to work a dance floor.

Taylor rolled her eyes. "Please don't tell that clown that. He will never sit down." They all made their way to the patio, to join in the fun.

#

The party was in full swing, and Jayden and Hannah were having a great time. Jayden found Andee and Tor. He introduced Hannah to them and wished them both well. They were just coming off the dance floor when Hannah whispered to Paige that she needed the ladies' room. Kissing Jayden, she let him know where she was headed.

Hannah had just exited the powder room when she bumped into Dain Sinclair. She was shocked to see him and was about to inquire as to why he was there, but Dain spoke first.

"What the hell are you doing here!" He asked, pissed. He forcefully grabbed Hannah by the arm.

"Hey! Let go of me," she exclaimed with anger of her own. Hannah snatched her arm from his grasp.

Jayden, coming to look for her, heard the exchange. He rounded the corner just as Dain grabbed Hannah a second time, trying to pull her away from any prying eyes.

Without warning, Jayden pulled him away from her and punched him in the face, knocking him into a nearby wall.

"What the hell are you doing manhandling her like that?" Jayden was furious. He couldn't believe Dain had put his hands on Hannah.

Hearing all the commotion, some of the partygoers who were inside the house, came to see what the ruckus was about. Anderson was first on the scene, with his wife and Taylor close behind.

"What's going on here?" Anderson asked of his brother and Dain. Holding Jayden, to keep him from hitting Dain a second time, Anderson asked again.

"This fool was manhandling Hannah," Jayden told his brother.

"Dain, what's going on?" This was from Taylor and she wasn't pleased with this scenario.

"I want to know why she's here," Dain demanded, as he nursed his rapidly swelling eye.

"What the hell business is it of yours why she's here? This is my brother's house…and if you must know, she came here with me!" Jayden told him. He was itching to knock his block off again.

"Dain, why is it any of your business?" Anderson repeated his brother's question. He had a feeling he wasn't going to like the answer and neither would Taylor.

Suddenly, all eyes turned to Dain, including Taylor who slowly folded her arms. She too was curious, as to why Dain found it necessary to interrogate the Stone's house guests.

But before he could speak, Taylor took a closer look at Hannah. She knew her from somewhere. Then it dawned on her. She was the woman from the restaurant, who warned her of Dain's reputation. Hannah was one of Dain's throwaways.

Sighing, Taylor spoke for Dain. "You're one of Dain's exes aren't you?" She asked. "You were the one who came to our table that night, to warn me about him, aren't you?" Hannah nodded.

By this time, Mia, Jayden and Anderson's sister, along with Kylon, Taylor's brother, had joined the crowd. Seeing the humor in the moment, Kylon couldn't help himself.

"Well Dain, just how many of your women do we have here tonight? Kylon chuckled.

Taylor shot her amused brother the evil eye, before turning her sights back on Dain.

Dain realized his mistake too late. If he had approached the situation differently, maybe he could have avoided all this.

"Look you guys, I'm sorry. I could have handled this better. And you all are right. I had no cause to question her. Hannah, Jayden I apologize." Dain hoped this was enough. He could see Jayden was geared up to hit him again.

"But you must admit, it is strange running up on you here," he added, speaking to Hannah.

Hannah only rolled her eyes. She never thought she would see this idiot again, let alone in Jayden's brother's home.

Taylor, not knowing what she felt about the whole situation, left the room, as did most of the guests who had gathered for the floor show.

Mia grasped Hannah's arm and escorted her into the kitchen for a stiff drink. She also had been on the receiving end of Dain's pump and dump.

"If I catch you putting your hands on my girl again, you will get more than a black eye next time," Jayden promised Dain. He still felt he owed Dain much more, for how he treated his sister. Having had his say, he went off to find Hannah.

"Well little brother," Dani told her twin, "you sure know how to break up a party. Someone had found Dani outside and informed her of her brother's troubles inside.

"Dain, what made you go off like that with Hannah in the first place?" Anderson asked him, annoyed. "Could it be a guilty conscience or do you have unfinished business with her? Whatever the reason, you better resolve it before you walk down the aisle to marry my cousin." Anderson shook his head before leaving to salvage Evan and Jean's party. Dani followed him, rolling her eyes at the trouble that seemed to follow her brother.

Dain found himself staring at the only person who decided to stick around—Taylor's brother Kylon.

"Anderson may not have stayed for the answers to those questions, but I need to know for my sister's sake," Kylon told him, all humor aside.

"It's simple," Dain sighed. "I saw her in a place I never expected to see her that's all. One of your former lovers shows up at a family gathering? I mean, come on. I didn't know she was with Jayden. You of all people should be able to understand, considering your girlfriend stalked me for months. I just thought it was another one of those situations."

"Dain my man. With all the women you have been through, you may want to start expecting this type of thing to happen more often than not. My only advice to you is this, don't hurt my sister. With that said, I am going back to join the party." Kylon left Dain to his thoughts.

#

"Oh my goodness Jayden, had I known Dain would be at that party, I never would have come," Hannah told him, as they drove to their hotel. They both had decided they'd had enough of Dain Sinclair for one night.

Jayden shook his head in the negative. "Oh no you don't. This is not your fault. He never should have put his hands on you," Jayden assured her, still angry. "So he's the asshole that played with your heart then drop-kicked you?"

Hannah sighed. "Unfortunately yes. If I thought for a second you knew him, I would have told you his name, and maybe we could have avoided all this." Hannah couldn't believe it. Out of all the people she could have run into that night, it had to be Dain Sinclair.

Jayden chuckled at first; then he started laughing so hard he had to pull over. Hannah looked at him as if he had gone insane. After he finally got a hold of himself. He shared the joke.

"Here I was all uptight over my reaction to seeing Andee and Tor together when it was your former boyfriend who caused all the drama. How strange is life, huh? Jayden chuckled at the irony.

"Jayden," Hannah said with a grin slowly spreading across her face.

"Hmm?" He asked as he pulled back onto the road.

"That was by far one of the best parties I have been invited to. All because I got to see Dain Sinclair get what was coming to him. She leaned over and kissed Jayden's cheek. "Thank you baby for the good time."

Jayden grinned.

#

No one needed to have worried about the party breaking up. Jean and Evan were still on the dance floor having the time of their lives. They had no idea what had transpired inside, as with most of the guests.

"Hey, where did you go to?" Devin asked Dani after she joined him at their table.

She rolled her eyes. "More of my brother's past life just caught up with him," she told him. "Jayden finally got a chance to pop him one," she continued, shaking her head.

"Because of Mia?"

"Nope, not this time. You know the woman Jayden brought with him, Hannah?" Devin nodded. "Well, she seems to be one of Dain's former 'girlfriends'. Dani raised her fingers, with air quotes. She gave him the rundown of what had taken place inside.

"Mmm, let me go get something to drink," she told Devin, after he shook his head in astonishment, over his soon-to-be brother-in-law and his antics. "I'll be right back.

Not finding what she wanted at the bar outside, Dani made her way to the backdoor just in time to catch a conversation between Tor and Evan. She was about to open the door when she heard Maalik's name mentioned.

"Well man, I'm glad nothing happened tonight. I really wanted Jean to get out and have a good time," Evan was telling Tor. "I'm glad my sister suggested this party, we both needed the stress reliever.

"I know what you mean. So there haven't been any more incidents of any kind?" Tor asked. He knew how much Evan wanted a piece of Nicolas. He just hoped he wouldn't take any unnecessary chances, to make that happen.

"No, none. Do you think he will try again?" Evan asked, genuinely concerned. Even though he would like to get his hands on Nicolas, he didn't want Jean in jeopardy.

"I don't know. But for sure, Maalik will be nearby just in case he does decide to try something else. He's had this house under surveillance from across the street since you and Jean arrived. We wanted to be prepared just in case he decided to show up here."

Dani's heart pounded. Could they be talking about Maalik Wyatt, her Maalik? The drink forgotten, she entered the house, strolling past the two men, straight to the bathroom instead.

Locking herself inside, Dani splashed water on her face. Her hand shook, as she reached for a paper towel. Patting her face dry, she stared at her reflection. They couldn't be talking about Maalik Wyatt. There had to be hundreds of Maaliks in the city alone, not to mention the state. But if that were true, why had she felt as if someone was watching her when she and Devin first arrived?

Dani carefully thought about the events, which led to her meeting Maalik. Did Devin hire him to find her? At the very least, he could have hired Tor. Which would mean Tor could have sent Maalik. With these thoughts, Dani didn't know if she should be happy or angry.

Thinking back on her encounter with Maalik, she believed he had no plans of seducing her. Fate had worked its magic on that situation. Dani breathed a sigh of relief. Maalik had set her away from him on the train because he was working for Tor. She believed he had no idea he would become attracted to her as she had him.

Thinking she needed to see him, to explain things to him, Dani pulled open the door to the bathroom. She was determined to march across the street to talk to him when Devin pulled her back to reality.

"Hey babe, the party is winding down. You about ready to leave?" He asked when she exited the bathroom. He was waiting for her.

Disappointed, Dani could only nod. After she and Devin said their goodbyes to their hosts, they made their way outside, along with the last of the stragglers. Walking across the street to their car, Dani fixated on the darkened driveway, where she was sure Maalik sat in the shadows. She took one last look as they drove past; wishing she could see him.

#

Maalik was stunned. He was more than sure Dani knew he was there, but how? He watched them through binoculars, as they exited the house and crossed the street. Dani looked directly into his eyes this time with awareness. Maalik almost dropped the binoculars, when he caught her staring back at him. He followed them through the field glasses, as they drove by, all the while with Dani fixated on him.

"How could she know," he whispered to himself. Not knowing what to think, Maalik slowly shook his head in wonder.

□

Chapter 34

The Gala

"Wow! Look at this place!" Jean exclaimed. She and Evan made their way into the ballroom. "This is far better than some stuffy old banquet with a dry chicken dinner," she further remarked. Jean was part of the planning committee that opted for a themed night for this year's gala.

She and Evan were attending Metro City's annual gala for special needs children. All of the city's major contributors were in attendance for the fundraiser, along with a few Hollywood celebrities. It appeared the themed event was a welcomed addition to the charity.

Instead of the usual mundane banquet atmosphere, the gala's committee wanted to bring some fun to the event. This year's theme featured the nineteen seventies. The hotel's ballroom had been transformed into a retro seventies lounge. The room drew its authentic appearance from plush seventies' styled sofas and period tables, that sported lava lamps, along with other seventies memorabilia. Displayed in the center of the dance floor was a huge mirrored disco ball, complete with strobing lights.

"I must say, when you told me about the theme, I never envisioned this. It is far more than you described," he told her. Evan marveled at the room's transformation, and the elaborate costumes some of the guests had chosen to wear.

Jean had chosen Evan's attire, which depicted him, as a replica of Richard Roundtree's *Shaft*. Evan sported a beige turtleneck, black polyester pants, and a brown leather jacket. Jean had completed the look with a short afro, sideburns, and sunglasses.

For her costume, she had chosen a pair of blue, hip-hugging bell bottoms, paired with a gold and brown paisley halter top. She too sported an afro that included a black-fisted hair pick in the back. In her lobes were large gold hoops that matched a gold spiral arm bracelet. For her feet, she chose a pair of brown suede platforms. Because of his height, Evan opted for a pair of low-heeled shoes, claiming platforms made him feel more of a giant with the added inches. Jean teased he was afraid he would trip and fall.

The couple moved further into the room; joining the other costumed guests. Not far behind, Maalik followed, wearing a white, vested suit, which looked as if he borrowed it from the movie Saturday Night Fever. He carefully scanned the throng of partygoers; making sure there wasn't more than fun lurking in the crowd. He had been following the Bennetts for days, with no other attempts made on Jean Bennett's life. He wondered if this could be just the venue the perpetrator looked for, to take another go at her.

As he searched the room, he caught sight of KT and Justin Graham. They too had dressed in costume for the night's festivities. KT wore zebra print bell bottoms, with a matching long-sleeved blouse that tied just below her full breasts, leaving her well-toned midriff bare. She chose not to wear a wig but sported her usual pixie style.

Maalik scrutinized KT a little longer. Still, he wondered. Did she have a hand in the attempts on Jean's life? He couldn't shake her uncanny resemblance to the woman on the motorcycle. And to make matters worse, she appeared to be conveniently unaccounted for, since the madness began. He didn't know much about KT, other than Tor seemed to trust her. For certain, the jury was still out on his personal opinion.

While KT appeared to be just another guest in the crowd, Maalik knew she carried her weapon in her white suede shoulder bag. He let his gaze linger a while longer, before turning back to the crowd. He would keep his eyes on her, as well as the others. It didn't matter to him that she was a supposed colleague.

#

KT glanced across the room at Maalik. She had been getting some unusual attention from him lately. At their last meeting with Tor, she caught him staring at her several times. She didn't know what his problem was, but if he persisted in his observation of her, she would have to confront him.

Turning her gaze back to her assignment, she watched Justin, move through the crowd; shaking hands with some of the other attendees. He had finally gotten rid of his cast and was in full Justin Graham mode; working the room for business. He should have had enough of that, after ending up married to Anastasia, she thought. Shaking her head, she turned her attention back to the costumed crowd. She was just about to move closer to Justin when she felt someone to her left. It was Detective Valero.

"Wow, nice costume," he complimented, as his eyes took in her figure. He had been watching her move about the room for a while and had decided to make his presence known.

"Thank you. You don't look half bad yourself," she commented.

Her eyes roamed his body from head to toe. He was decked out in some of Ron O'Neal's best Super Fly attire, complete with wide wide-brimmed hat.

"Well you know, I had to blend in," he told her with a grin.

"I was unaware you would be here tonight," KT said, still observing the room.

"Actually, I've contributed to this charity from the very beginning, so I always attend the galas. Because of the trouble with Justin, this is the first time that I'll be working, instead of enjoying the festivities."

"Well, this is my first one, and I must say it is very detailed. Are all the galas put together like this one?" She asked him, returning her gaze to Justin.

Eric shook his head. "No, this is the first themed one, and I must say it turned out great. I hope they continue with the themes. This is so much better than the sit-down banquets we usually have."

KT nodded her agreement. "Well detective, I better get a handle on Mr. Graham. He's getting a little bit too relaxed with this crowd. Excuse me."

KT wandered off to catch up with Justin. Although the room seemed safe enough, she felt no one could predict when danger would pop out of the woodwork.

Eric watched her make her way to Justin's side. His eyes lingered on her shapely behind, until it disappeared into the crowd. He drew a hand down his face, as he turned back to his task of surveilling the guests.

"When this is over..." he trailed off. He had been thinking about KT since he met her. He planned to know her much better, once the case was resolved.

Chapter35

Veda Cross

With the most popular music of the seventies, pumping out through the speakers, the guests were in full party mode. Most had gathered on the dance floor to do the Hustle. Some were even doing the robot, which brought laughter to many.

Among those who were not on the floor was Veda Cross, a self-invited guess. Veda had worried she may have a problem getting into the gala since entrance required an invitation. However, the male attendants at the door took one look at her pushed-up breasts, along with her generous behind, in a pair of red leather hot pants, and they let her in without a problem. Veda blended right into the crowd, with her carefully chosen seventies' attire.

Circling the room, but staying close to the shadows, she sought out her first target of the night—Justin Graham. Once she spotted him, she also spotted the bitch who almost caught her in the yard the night she took a shot at him. Turning from her target, Veda searched the room for an opportunity.

#

Maalik circled the ballroom, paying close attention to anything or anyone out of the ordinary. Everyone seemed to be enjoying the night's event and weren't concerned with any danger. He had just made his way to the front of the ballroom when Dani entered—alone.

Dani was dressed in an orange flowered mini dress with knee-high, brown suede Go-go boots. She had covered her hair with an Afro-puff wig. Although she looked decidedly different, he would have known her anywhere. His heart pounded wildly, as he watched her greet various people, all the while moving through the crowded room. He followed her to the bar.

"Can I get you something to drink Miss?" the bartender asked her.

"Yes, a Merlot please," she told the woman.

Dani hadn't wanted to attend this year's gala. She didn't feel up to it. However, since Paige was close to her delivery date, Anderson didn't think they should attend. With Devin out of town on business, and Andee spending time with her husband, this left her to represent her and Paige's business, *Beautiful Colors Designs,* alone.

Dani accepted her drink, while she observed the costume-clad people on the dance floor. They appeared to be having a great time. She looked around, admiring the decorated room. It did give her the feeling of being in a nightclub from the chosen decade.

"Ms. Sinclair," Maalik greeted her. Dani turned at the sound of his voice.

"Maalik…How are you?" She asked, after searching her mind for a better greeting. Although she'd known he was at the Stone's party, she didn't think she would find him at this one.

"I'm good. Where is Devin?" He asked, looking around the room for his presence. He secretly hoped he wasn't there.

"He's out of town on business. Maalik, I want to apologize for the way things ended in Toronto," she quickly added. If she didn't get a chance to say anything else to him that night, she wanted to apologize.

"I...I understand Dani, I do. You thought things were over with you and Devin. After you told me your story, I understood why you ran away from him. And like him, I wouldn't have let that stop me from being with you. He's your man, I get it. Besides, we were two consenting adults, remember?"

Although Maalik did understand why things ended for them in Toronto, his heart didn't feel the same. He would not burden her with his issues. She didn't deserve that.

"Dani, I want to explain the real reason I was in Toronto..." Maalik started.

"I know why you were there Maalik. I put it together after I overheard Tor and Evan discussing your surveillance across the street from the Stones. So you don't have to explain." She smiled.

"Ah, so you did know I was there when you were staring at me," he remarked. Dani nodded.

"Maalik, I…" Dani never got a chance to finish her sentence.

Suddenly, there were screams, as a struggle ensued several yards from them. This quickly caught Maalik's attention. However, he didn't move towards the commotion. His concentration immediately shifted from the melee near the dance floor to something across the room.

Dani watched Maalik's expression change, as something caught his eye. Before she knew it, he was rushing to the other side of the ballroom. She watched, as he quickly followed two women heading towards the ladies' room.

She realized he was on the job. Dani wanted to tell him she missed him and that she couldn't stop thinking about their time together, but fate had stepped in once again to prevent it. Not knowing or caring what was happening with the uproar on the dance floor, she took a last look towards the ladies' room before she left. There wasn't anything more to say. She would be marrying Devin at the end of the month.

#

Anastasia Stanton-Graham had watched while her husband worked the ballroom. She was beside herself with rage. Not only had he not returned home to her, he had moved another woman into his house.

She had been slipping in and out of town for weeks, each time circling his house, only to find that an attractive woman seemed to be living there with him. She had contemplated what her next move should be when she wrangled an invitation to the gala. Anastasia knew Justin would be there. He never missed an opportunity to glad hand, plus this was one of his favorite charities.

Moving closer to him and his bimbo, she took in the woman. Anastasia found her to be more than just attractive, the woman was devastatingly gorgeous. Having had enough, she took a knife from her purse and plowed through the crowd towards her husband, screaming, "You bastard", all the way.

Plunging the weapon forward, she was able to catch him in the forearm; the same arm that had been broken, before KT was able to wrestle her to the ground.

#

Veda had been watching the crowd carefully, trying to decide how best to get next to Justin. As she examined the throng of people for an opportunity, she spotted a person she never expected to see, Anastasia Stanton-Graham. Veda wondered what she was doing there. She was supposed to be back in North Carolina. Veda watched Anastasia run up to Justin, screaming like a lunatic. This was not the plan.

"What is this crazy bitch doing? She's ruining everything!" Veda watched in disbelief as Anastasia stabbed Justin Graham.

Too late to stop her, Veda searched the room for her second target of the night.

She smiled when she spotted Jean standing alone, enthralled with Anastasia's foolishness. After Anastasia's stunt, everyone rushed to the scene, including Evan, Jean's husband. Slowly making her way to her target, she pulled the small caliber handgun from her purse. Coming up behind Jean, Veda leveled the pistol at her back.

"This is a gun in your back lady...I want you to walk slowly to the powder room." Veda poked her with the tip of the weapon.

Not knowing what else to do, Jean did as she was told.

#

Anastasia screamed and thrashed, with KT pinning her to the floor, while Detective Valero handcuffed her. Another undercover officer hustled Justin out through a service exit, to be transported to a nearby hospital.

After Anastasia was placed in a squad car, to be carted off to jail, Detective Valero made his way back to KT.

"Are you okay? She didn't hurt you, did she?"

Eric had spotted Anastasia charging towards Justin and KT. Unfortunately, he was on the other side of the ballroom and was helpless in stopping her. KT saw her seconds before she stabbed Justin. She had shoved him just as Anastasia reached them, enabling her to pierce his arm instead of her true target, his heart.

"I'm fine, this isn't my blood," she told him of the blood that covered her face and neck. "Is Justin going to be okay?" She retrieved a napkin, from a nearby table, to remove Justin's blood.

Eric nodded. "It wasn't too deep, he'll be just fine. Although I don't think he's too happy it's the same arm that just healed," he surmised.

"So, I guess we were all correct. Anastasia Stanton-Graham was out to kill her husband," Eric added. "What's the matter?" He asked KT, after catching her puzzled expression.

"Eric, I know for certain she wasn't in town on the other attempts." There has to be someone else involved in this," she told him. Before Eric could respond, there was more trouble.

"My wife…my wife is missing!" This was Evan. After the commotion with Justin had died down, he had gone back to where he left Jean, only to find one of her earrings on the floor instead. Jean was gone.

At this new round of shouts, KT and Eric turned their attention to Evan.

"When did you see her last?" Eric asked him.

"She was right here. I told her to stay put, while I went to see what was going on with Justin. When I came back, she was gone and this was on the floor." He held one of his wife's earrings.

Detective Valero called to one of his men to seal off the building. He hoped she hadn't left the complex.

KT looked around for Maalik. He was nowhere to be found. The last time she saw him, he was talking to a woman with afro-puffs. He was supposed to be watching Jean Bennett.

"What the hell is going on?" She whispered to herself. Checking her purse for her gun, she took off in search of Jean and Maalik.

#

Maalik's gaze swung in Jean's direction, just in time to see a woman move to her side. Seconds later, he watched the blood drain from Jean Bennett's face. At that moment, Dani was forgotten. Without saying a word, he reached for his gun, holstered underneath his jacket, and hurried after Jean and the mystery woman.

Veda Cross shoved Jean into the bathroom. She knew she only had a small window of time before someone would notice Jean was missing. With Anastasia's stunt, she wouldn't be able to collect on Justin's bounty, so she would have to make do with finishing her assignment with Jean.

"What are you doing? What is it that you want? Jean asked the woman. She didn't know her and couldn't understand what the woman could possibly want with her.

"Miss, this isn't personal, just business," Veda informed her, while she attached a silencer to her gun.

"Business? What business? I don't understand." Jean was frightened. She never should have allowed this woman to remove her from the ballroom. Would Evan find her before it was too late?

"Look, I don't have time to explain it to you. Just know that this is all your ex-husband's doing," Veda told her.

"Nicolas? I...I don't understand!" Jean was confused. Did Nicolas hate her so much that he wanted her dead?

Just then, Maalik quietly made his way into the bathroom. Veda, with her back to him, never saw him enter. With his gun raised, he placed it behind the woman's right ear.

"Slowly lower the gun," he told her.

Startled, Veda turned, intent on shooting Maalik, only to have him twist her arm behind her back, forcing her to drop the gun. A frightened, but relieved Jean, ran from the ladies' room, right into Evan's arms. He was accompanied by Detective Valero and KT, who rushed past them to help apprehend the woman who had taken her.

"Baby, are you alright?" He asked his shaking wife. Evan wanted to kick himself for leaving her alone. With the night's joyous festivities, he had become too trusting and let his guard down. He also made the mistake of thinking the attempt on Justin's life, was the only threat in the ballroom that night.

"Baby please forgive me, I will never leave you again," he told her. Evan held her tightly, while the police escorted the woman from the building. He hoped the nightmare was finally over.

#

"Mrs. Bennett, did the woman say anything to you? Why she wanted to kill you?" Detective Valero asked her. After the paramedic's assessment, and Jean had calmed down, she was being questioned, to try and make some sense, as to why someone wanted her dead.

"She said that it was business and it was all due to Nicolas," she told Eric.

"And Nicolas is…?

"Nicolas Hampton, her ex-husband," Evan spoke for her. He was fuming. He knew Nicolas was behind this, and he wanted to know why. Why go to these lengths to hire someone? Evan filled Eric in on the night they returned home to find Nicolas waiting along with all of the incidents that occurred afterward and his suspicions of the culprit, after the first incident.

"Please tell me you're going to arrest that guy tonight. As long as he's running around loose, my wife's life is still in danger."

"We'll pick him up, but it will only be the woman's word against his unless she has some evidence to say otherwise," Eric informed them. "Excuse me, folks." Detective Valero spoke into his radio, placing an all-points bulletin for Nicolas Hampton.

"Look detective, if you want us, we will be at our home in San Francisco. We're not going to stay another minute in this city until you can place that guy behind bars," Evan told him. Taking Jean's hand, he led her from the ballroom with Maalik following close behind.

Maalik sighed. Looks like he was going to San Francisco. His work was not finished until the case was completely solved. He just hated he didn't get a chance to finish his conversation with Dani. As he left the ballroom, he looked around to see if she had stayed behind. Not seeing her, he sighed again, in frustration.

KT, watching Eric wrap up his interview with the Bennetts, was still puzzled by the second person who was involved in Justin's case. What was she missing? Will Anastasia name her accomplice? She had questions, but no answers. Frustrated, she left the hotel to join Justin at the hospital. Although he was surrounded by police, like Maalik, she knew her job wasn't finished either.

☐

Chapter 36

Veda Cross

Veda Cross paced the length of the holding cell. She was trying to reason her way out of this mess. Dropping onto the hard, metal bench, she bit her lip. She realized she had been caught in the act, with no way out, unless she made a deal. She may not be able to avoid jail time, but she may be able to shorten it substantially. Quickly weighing her options, she came to a decision.

"Officer!" She yelled.

#

Veda Cross stared at the floor, while she waited for someone in authority to get around to her. Out of all the jobs she had done over the years, she had never been caught. She and her cousin Freddy had moved across the country, establishing businesses in nearly every major city. Most of the time, they had to muscle their way into the larger venues, which always brought a change in the street climate. And with any change, came conflict. That's where she came in.

Whenever there were problems with the competition, she was the one to handle it. The enemy never saw it coming. Who was looking for a ditsy female stripper to take them out?

Veda Cross, aka Lucinda Matthews, stripper extraordinaire, had the perfect cover. With her long wigs, airhead appearance, and curvy body, she would lure the unsuspecting men into the VIP rooms, to showcase her special talents. After they were taken, for either their money or their lives, she would move on to the next dupe. She and Freddy had cleaned up.

Veda smirked when she thought about Nicolas Hampton. The guy never knew what hit him. After she worked her charms on him, he'd lost everything. Her smirk quickly turned into a frown, after recalling how she had gotten herself into this mess. If Freddy hadn't been so greedy, she wouldn't be sitting in a jail cell.

Veda lifted her head when she heard the officer unlock the cell door.

"Veda Cross, come with me. Detective Valero will see you now," the female officer informed her. Veda prepared herself to face her fate.

Chapter 37

Detective Valero

After speaking with Veda Cross, aka Lucinda Matthews, Eric Valero rounded up all those who were involved, except one person. He was sure to have everyone in custody by the end of the day.

He shook his head at the tangled mess Veda Cross had unraveled. He would not have guessed the two attempted murder cases were related. One was out of loyalty and protection; the other, because of good old greed.

They picked up Nicolas Hampton soon after Veda Cross was arrested. Eric had been certain he was the one who put the hit out on Alfra-Jean Bennett. However, after Veda's confession, it became clear there was much more to the plan than met the eye.

Valero turned, at Maalik, KT, and Justin entering the observation room.

"How's the arm?" Eric asked, gesturing towards Justin's freshly bandaged left arm which was now in a sling. The arm that had been broken on the first attempt on his life.

Justin raised his stitched arm with a grimace. "I think I'll live," he told his friend.

Eric's gaze shifted from Justin to KT. She was staring intently at the woman on the other side of the glass. The woman was about her height and build, with nearly the same haircut; however, the similarities stopped there. Veda Cross was not only darker, but she had a seemingly sleazy demeanor. The woman carried herself like a hood rat. Even in a prison jumpsuit, she still managed to come off cheap.

Maalik also noted the similarities. The two women were so close in build, that he had suspected KT of living a double life. The two even owned similar motorcycles.

"Did you get anything out of my wife?" Justin asked Eric, breaking the room's silence.

When they first brought Anastasia in, she was enraged she hadn't killed Justin. She was determined to put an end to him after she assumed he was sleeping with his house guest. When she first came to town, she was prepared to lure Justin back to North Carolina for reconciliation. But after observing KT come and go from his home as she pleased, she wanted revenge. She thought Justin was having an affair and had left her for the woman.

Rubbing his fingers across his mustache, Eric shook his head. "Before her actions last night, she swears she knows nothing about a contract on you."

"How is that possible, if she was the only one with a motive? Not to mention, *she* was the one who tried to stab him to death," KT interjected.

"I didn't know what to make of it at first, but as you will see in a minute, it will all become clear," he assured her.

"Ok, you said you rounded up everyone involved in Jean Bennett's case. So does that mean Hampton has been arrested?" Maalik asked. He had been all set to accompany Evan and Jean to San Francisco until Tor volunteered to escort them. He wanted Maalik in town, in case Nicolas wasn't found. Tor believed Maalik could be a resource in his capture.

"Yes, along with our favorite neighborhood thug, Fye Freddy," Valero told him.

Maalik nodded. "I knew that guy was in it up to his short neck. Especially after spotting Nicolas Hampton coming out of his house. That's where I followed this woman to," he told the group; gesturing at Veda with a nod of his head.

"Detective, Mrs. Graham's father is here." One of the uniformed officers stuck his head into the room to inform him.

Eric nodded. "Put him in interview room two, then bring in his daughter."

"I take it the old man came to bail his precious baby out of jail," Justin commented with a frown.

Eric switched on a monitor, which showed Roland Stanton being escorted into an interview room next, to Veda's.

"I think you will find this very interesting," he informed Justin.

Picking up a file from the table, Detective Valero left the observation room. The group watched him enter the second interview room, just as Anastasia Stanton-Graham was being brought in. Seeing her father, she fell into his arms, sobbing loudly.

"Baby girl, it's going to be alright. I am going to get you out of here and hire the best attorneys money can buy," Roland Stanton consoled his weeping daughter.

"I think, while you're at it, you may want to hire one or two for yourself," Eric suggested. He watched the older man's back stiffen at his recommendation.

All three, in the observation room, looked at each other perplexed at this statement.

"What do you mean?" Roland gruffly asked the detective.

"Why don't you both sit down," Eric told the pair, before handing Anastasia a box of tissues. He waited until she had gotten herself under control before he continued.

"Mr. Stanton, you really shouldn't have used thugs and strippers to do your dirty work," Eric told Roland. "As soon as they were caught, they turned on everyone."

"Listen here son, I don't know what the hell you're talking about," Roland Stanton responded with indignation.

"Don't you? It appears that a colleague of mine followed the money trail right back to you." Eric paused to see if Roland would give up on his pretense.

"Still no answer? Ok." Eric sighed. "I guess I will have to lay it out for you and your daughter. But before I do, just to cross all the T's and dot all the I's, you have the right to remain silent…" Eric read Roland Stanton his Miranda rights, while the curious group in the observation room looked on.

"Now, with that behind us…you see Mr. Stanton, a private investigator stumbled upon your corporation's involvement with quite a few shady dealings and companies. One of them being Fye Freddy's strip club Caitee Cat's Lair."

"It appears that your company, Stan-Con Global, wasn't built on the up and up, but was built on the foundation of organized crime. It also seems, Mr. Stanton, that you are one of the biggest crime bosses on the East Coast.

"But I digress," Eric said.

He laid the foundation, more so for the audience in the other room than for Stanton and his daughter. Although, it appeared this was the first time Anastasia Stanton-Graham had heard of any of it. She let her gaze drift between Eric and her father, fully astonished.

"You hired Fye Freddy to kill your son-in-law. Didn't you?" He asked him.

"Daddy? Is what he's saying true?" Anastasia asked. Her head was swimming with this new information. Is her father a gangster? And he plotted to have Justin killed?

The shock in the other room was just as explosive. They all had assumed this was all Anastasia's doing. No one even suspected anyone else.

Roland Stanton stared off into space. Refusing to acknowledge anything that the detective had said. He wouldn't even look at his daughter.

"Daddy, look at me! Is what he's saying true?" She asked him again, this time pulling out of his embrace, to look him in his eyes. Roland didn't respond.

"It doesn't matter if you answer or not. We have all the evidence we need to put you away," Eric informed him.

"And oh…by the way. You may want to get a whole team of attorneys because when we're done with you, the Federal government will want their piece." Eric gathered his files and exited the room, leaving the father and daughter alone.

Anastasia was in disbelief. She had no idea her family's fortune was built on such treachery. Not knowing anything else to say, after her father refused to tell her the truth, she called for the officer to take her back to her cell.

After Anastasia was taken away, another officer came for a still-defiant Roland Stanton. He snatched away from the officer, as the man escorted him from the interview room to his waiting cell.

Justin was slowly shaking his head at this turn of events. He never thought his father-in-law was involved. Although, Roland had quietly warned him after the wedding, that he would pay if he ever did anything to upset his daughter. He just assumed it was an empty threat. Now he knew differently.

"So, Fye Freddy hired Veda or Lucinda…or whoever she is, to kill Justin? KT asked Eric when he came back into the room. She had been flipping through his files.

"Yes. Freddy doesn't get his hands dirty. He always hires the workout. And it seems, to the same woman." Eric pointed to the interview room, where Veda Cross still sat.

"I did some digging and found that Ms. Cross is Freddy's cousin. They had a very lucrative scam going at most of his strip clubs," he told the group.

"You see Ms. Cross there, has a unique talent that seems to get some of their customers in trouble. Once a customer is wowed by her, it makes it easy for her and Freddy to help the poor fool to part with his money."

"What's the unique talent?" Maalik asked, with KT and Justin nodding in agreement.

Eric sat on the corner of a table grinning, before he continued.

"It seems Veda can pick up objects with her vagina and make them disappear and reappear at will," he told the stunned room. He chuckled at their reactions.

"Ok, I'll bite, what was the scam?" KT asked, after getting over her stunned amazement.

"Well Luscious Lucinda, as she's known in the stripper world, would charge a couple of grand in the VIP room for her special talent. First using objects, such as a beer bottle. Then after the client saw what she could do, she would charge a few thousand more, without using a bottle, if you know what I mean."

"And like with anything, someone always gets hooked. Returning night after night to visit her," Eric continued. "If the guy is hooked enough, he will do anything for her. Give her money, jewels, you name it. And because Fye Freddy runs an illegal betting operation inside the clubs, they usually place bets to try to double their money to keep Lucinda happy."

Justin shook his head in amazement. "And my father-in-law helped fund this little operation?"

Eric nodded. "Roland Stanton seeded Freddy's string of clubs. He got a cut from every operation, in every club Freddy owned, with illegal gambling being the biggest profit.

"And Maalik, this is where your case comes into play. By chance or by bad luck, Nicolas Hampton ran across Luscious Lucinda. And weak-minded as he is, got pulled into the game. He started betting with Freddy until he lost and lost big. Owing Freddy more than seventy-five grand."

"This is why he slinked back to his ex-wife, hoping she would take him back, so he could get his hands on her money. Lucinda was the one who was pushing for this, after one night of Nicolas bragging about how he had come into his money in the first place. Lucinda figured he could get more from Jean Bennett."

"But she didn't take him back, so how was killing her going to profit Freddy?" Maalik asked. "Was it revenge against Nicolas?"

"No." Eric shook his head. "After the first plan didn't work, Freddy stumbled upon a quarter of a million dollar insurance policy on Mrs. Bennett. Nicolas had taken it out while they were married. He put the policy away and had forgotten about it. But Freddy's goons, in the process of searching his place for anything valuable, came across said policy and forced him to sign it over."

"So Freddy hired Veda to take care of Jean to collect on the policy." Justin finished for him. Eric nodded.

"There are a lot of unsolved disappearances and murders in cities these two have frequented. So I am sure with Ms. Cross' help, some of these mysteries will be cleared up. That is, if she cooperates with the Feds. She's made a deal with our DA for a shorter sentence, but I don't think she realizes crossing state lines, puts her in a bigger hot seat. At any rate, Freddy and his cousin will be put away for quite some time," Eric assured them.

"Wow." Maalik was overwhelmed.

"KT, it was your lead that led Tor to follow up in North Carolina," Eric told her. "When you told him about Fye Freddy visiting Stan-Con, he did some digging and found the corruption link to the company. At the time, Tor still believed Freddy was working for Anastasia."

"It took some digging to unravel all the dummy corporations and paper trails, to link it back to Roland instead. Only with Freddy's help, I might add. He told us where to look, without actually giving Roland away."

"So, Nicolas didn't actually put the hit out on his ex-wife…" Maalik commented.

"No, he didn't. But he knew there was a hit and didn't stop it. He also provided Freddy with information about her hypersensitivity to nuts, which Freddy passed on to Veda. So he will be charged with conspiracy." Eric answered.

"So that pretty much wraps everything up on both cases. Your clients are safe again," he told KT and Maalik.

Maalik held up a finger to get their attention. "Umm, I think I owe you an apology KT," he told her.

"Don't tell me…you thought I had gone over to the dark side?" She asked. She now understood why she was getting scrutiny from Maalik. After seeing Veda Cross, she could understand why he might think that.

"You're forgiven," she told him. "But don't ever let that happen again," she added, with a grin that surprised the men.

"Another question, did Nicolas know Veda was the hit woman?" Justin asked.

Eric shook his head. "No. Nicolas only knew her as Lucinda. He had planned to get enough money together to take her to Las Vegas, not knowing she would disappear on him the moment he was broke. When he couldn't get Freddy's money, from his ex-wife, Lucinda stopped coming around. He just assumed she had found deeper pockets. He was shocked to find out how he had been duped."

"Well, it looks like he got what was coming to him," Justin said. "I never liked Jean much, but I hear she has made some changes in her life, so she didn't deserve that idiot wreaking havoc on her." Justin just shook his head at the twisted turn of events.

"I think it's about time I call the Bennetts and let them know that all is well. I know Andee will be glad, so Tor can come home." Maalik said his goodbyes and left.

"I should be going too. I need to fly to North Carolina and see about my daughter. Now that her mother is in jail, I'm all she has." Justin was wondering how he was going to manage with Cara. He hadn't been in her life much, because of her mother.

"Before I go, I want to thank you KT, for saving my life." Justin shook her hand and left.

"This has been an enlightening day," KT told Eric after everyone left. "I would never have thought these cases were remotely related. Wonders never cease."

"You know, I'm really glad your case is over," Eric told her.

"And why is that Detective?"

"So I can do this." Eric pulled KT into his arms and kissed her.

☐

Chapter 38

Justin

Before Justin left the police station, he asked to see his wife. While he waited, he marveled at the events that brought them to this point. He never loved Anastasia and she never loved him. He couldn't understand why she would try to harm him. Her father, on the other hand, warned him. Although he never could have conceived these people, either of them, was capable of murder.

Justin closed his eyes, thinking about his part in the whole mess. If he hadn't been so ambitious, in such a hurry to make it to the top, he would never have slept with Anastasia in the first place. He conceded that his greed had set the chain of events into motion. The first casualty being his relationship with Paige, right down to the attempts on his life. If he could just go back in time and change things.

The door opened and an officer brought a handcuffed Anastasia into the small room. After seating her, the female sergeant stood at a distance to give them some privacy.

After studying his emotionally crushed wife for a long while, Justin finally spoke. "I don't know what to say to you, Anastasia. Why did you try to kill me? Why couldn't you just give me a divorce and let us part ways without all of this?" Justin gestured at the entire situation, along with her confinement. "We never loved each other, so I don't understand."

"Our wedding vows," she stated just above a whisper.

Justin was puzzled. "What about them?"

"In your vows to me, you said you would love me, cherish me," she told him.

Justin thought Anastasia was slowly slipping from reality. "Anastasia, those were just words. Part of the charade we played out for your family and friends. They didn't mean anything. You know that. Those words meant about as much as yours to me." He couldn't believe they were having this conversation. She knew, during the entire ceremony, he was thinking of Paige, not her.

Anastasia sighed heavily. Although she knew their marriage was a sham, she still wanted the fairy tale. She wanted him to make the words true.

Her entire childhood had been filled with nannies, maids, and chauffeurs. Her parents never had time for her. When they weren't giving parties or flying off to some remote destination, they were sending her off to boarding school. So when she chose Justin for her husband, she hoped he would learn to love her. But now she knew that was impossible because she didn't know how to love herself.

"What's going to happen to Cara? With daddy going off to prison and me…" she trailed off.

Staring off in a daze, she continued. "The police say the Feds will take away all of our money, because of daddy's criminal activity. We're broke. I don't know what my mother is going to do." Anastasia began to sob, as reality finally hit home for her.

"You don't have to worry about Cara. She's my daughter and I will take care of her," he assured her. He knew he and the child would have some rough days, especially after being under Anastasia's constant care, but he would manage.

With Justin's assurance of care for their daughter, they both sat in silence; both engrossed in their thoughts. Neither of them knew what the future would bring after this.

"I think I should go. Do you need anything?" Justin finally asked.

Anastasia, wiping away tears, shook her head.

Justin got up from the table. But before he left, he leaned over and kissed her forehead. Although he didn't love her, he hated seeing her in this condition. As he reached for the door, her words stopped him.

"Justin, I won't contest the divorce. Just send me the papers and I will sign them. I will also give up my parental rights to Cara."

Without facing her, Justin nodded and left his sobbing wife.

Chapter 39

The Bennetts

Evan ended the call with Maalik. He breathed a sigh of relief that all parties involved in his wife's case were in custody. His Jean was safe. Evan learned, that although Nicolas Hampton was the catalyst for all the drama, he was not the one who was trying to kill her.

"Baby, who was that on the phone," Jean asked her husband.

Pulling her into his arms, he kissed her. "That was Maalik," he gladly informed her, along with Tor, who was staring out the window.

"Tor, Maalik had some great news. Nicolas, along with the others involved are behind bars."

"You're safe baby." Evan smiled before kissing her again. This time with passion and joy.

"What happened?" Jean wanted to know.

She had only learned of the plot against her after Veda Cross tried to kill her. Evan had no choice, but to explain everything on the flight back to San Francisco. Jean was shocked, then angry with her husband for keeping the information from her. She reasoned that had she known, she would have been more cautious at the gala.

Jean hadn't stayed angry with Evan long. How could she? She realized he was only trying to protect her the best way he knew how.

While Evan sat Jean down to explain what Maalik told him, Tor called Maalik himself. After speaking with him, he phoned KT, to get the details in her case. Tor heaved a sigh of amazement at what his two employees had to tell him. However, he was glad to know it was all over and he could go home. Tapping his phone again, he dialed his wife to tell her he would be home soon.

"I will leave you two newlyweds alone," Tor told the couple. "I've called for a car to take me to the airport."

"Man, after all you've done for us, the least I could do is give you a ride to the airport," Evan told his friend.

Tor shook his head. "Not a problem. I know you two have better things to do instead of babysitting me." Tor winked.

"Tor, thank you so much, for everything," Jean told him, pulling him into a hug.

"Yeah, man. Thanks for everything." Evan clasped his shoulder, as a notification sounded on Tor's phone, indicating his Uber had arrived.

"Well, that's for me. You two take care." Tor grabbed his bag and left.

"Ok, Mr. Bennett, now that the danger has passed and we have the house to ourselves again, what shall we do with all of this free time?" Jean asked her husband.

Without saying a word, Evan picked up his little woman, and slung her over his shoulder, heading for their bedroom.

☐

Chapter 40

Maalik

Maalik stood outside Dani's house, not sure if he
should ring the bell. He had sat in his truck for a good thirty
minutes before getting out, to make the trek up the street.
Although he knew Devin was out of town on business, and
wouldn't be back for a couple of days, he still didn't want
his truck parked near her home.

He contemplated coming to her after leaving the
police station but got cold feet. Besides, he had paperwork
to finish on the Bennett case. Also, he promised Tor he
would pick him up from the airport, to discuss the case's
completion, which worked out to his advantage.

Needing to see Dani again, he carefully picked Tor,
to learn if Devin was indeed still out of town. Maalik knew
he wasn't in town the night before, because Dani had
attended the gala alone. He learned Devin would be gone
for a few more days, thus allowing him to visit her. After
arriving at her address, he needed a push to ring her
doorbell.

"Since you've made it this far, you may as well go all the way," he mumbled to himself. Maalik pressed the bell before he lost his nerve. Only a few seconds passed before the door was opened.

"Maalik?" Dani asked after she pulled the door open to find him on the other side.

"I had to see you. Dani…I felt there were some things that we left unsaid," he cautiously told her. He was still uncertain, as to whether he should have come.

Dani stepped aside to allow him entrance. Closing the door behind her, she led him into her media room, where she had been trying to watch a television show. Trying, because her mind continued to drift to Maalik; wishing she could see him again. She wondered if her thoughts had conjured him up.

"Have you eaten…would you like something to drink?" She asked. Dani was overjoyed to find him standing on her doorstep. She too, felt some things needed to be said.

"No, I'm good," he told her. She gestured for him to sit. Maalik took a seat on the oversized sofa, with Dani sitting next to him.

Clearing his throat, he spoke. "First, I want to apologize for racing off last night at the gala. I was there to protect Jean Bennett and well…"

Dani nodded. "I understand. I read what happened on the local news site this morning," she told him. And for the parts the article didn't report, Paige had filled her in on the rest.

Maalik looked around the room, searching his mind for words to say. He'd rehearsed what he would say to her while outside, but after being in her presence, all thought was lost.

"Maalik, why are we acting as if we're strangers?" She asked. "We were more comfortable with each other when we *were* actual strangers on the train to Toronto."

Maalik grinned. "You know, you're right. I shouldn't be this wound up. Oh, is it okay that I'm here? I mean you didn't know I was coming or anything and…"

Maalik was babbling. Dani mentally shook her head, realizing she would have to be the one to take control and break the ice.

Without warning, she took his face into the palms of her hands. Drawing him to her, she kissed him. This was all the consent Maalik needed. He parted her lips with his tongue, deepening the kiss. Needing to feel her body against his, he pulled her under him, as he coaxed her backward, onto the sofa.

While Maalik sat outside in his truck, deciding if he should visit her, Dani had prepared herself for the night alone. Not expecting any visitors, she was dressed only in a tee shirt and panties. When her doorbell rang, she grabbed her robe, intending to pull it on as she made her way to the door. But once she saw Maalik on the security monitor, she tossed it on a nearby chair, forgetting it once he was inside.

Reaching under her tee, Maalik ripped the panties from her body. He hurriedly pulled the shirt over her head, tossing it to the floor. Hungrily, he lowered his mouth to her plump breasts, suckling her nipples, as his fingers found their destination. His hands were touching her everywhere at once.

Not satisfied with the confinements of the couch, he got up to push a table out of his way. After making sure they had enough room on the rug-covered floor, Maalik pulled her there with him. He didn't think they could make it to a bed.

Undressing himself quickly, he donned a condom seconds, before he entered her; thrusting inside of her feverishly. All Dani could do was hold on, as Maalik made it his mission to top their joining in Toronto. He rode her with a passion that even he couldn't understand, with both crying out at the overpowering sensations that rippled through their bodies.

Just when Dani didn't think she could handle more, Maalik exploded. Breathing heavily, he rolled off of her, trying to catch his breath. Dani's body shook, as multiple orgasms vibrated through her. She was stunned at the intensity of their joining.

Finally able to speak, Maalik voiced what he was feeling. "OH MY GOD…what was that?" he asked. He too was stunned at what just happened. Never had he experienced anything so powerful.

"I don't know Maalik…but, could you do it again? Dani asked with a wicked grin.

Happy to oblige the lady, Maalik reached for another condom.

☐

Chapter 41

Devin

Devin Powers massaged his temples while watching Maalik Wyatt leave his fiancée's home, in the early hours of the morning. He observed him, from his rearview mirror, as he crossed the street and lumbered to his truck. Devin had been sitting in his rental all night.

He had noticed something was wrong with Dani the moment they got back from Toronto. She had been restless, unable to sleep. She should have been on cloud nine, after agreeing to marry him. He certainly was. He was about to marry the woman of his dreams.

He tried to chalk Dani's mood up to being tired from her trip. Devin even rationalized, she may have been a little uncomfortable about him knowing her secret. A secret she had no trouble telling a stranger—Maalik.

From the start, he felt there may have been something between the two, but she hadn't gotten any unusual phone calls and they spent every night they were back together. But still, something was amiss. He could feel it.

Devin soon received the confirmation that he wasn't imagining things. His world collapsed around him one night when they were making love. Dani called him Maalik. At that moment, he knew for sure she and Maalik had been together in Toronto. Dani never realized she had given away her secret with that small slip of the tongue.

Not knowing what to do, he decided not to say anything about the blunder. He had to think. Did she not love him anymore? Was that the only time they had been together? Would she see him again? These were the questions that kept him awake.

Devin wanted to know just what was going on between Dani and Maalik Wyatt, so he formed a plan. He told Dani he would be out of town for a few days. In reality, Devin never left the city. Instead, he decided to rent a car and follow her.

The first couple of days, there wasn't anything and he began to believe he had made a mistake. That was until the night of the gala. He followed Dani there, where he observed her talking to Maalik. He noted how they looked at each other, and their body language. He didn't get to watch them long, before Maalik ran off across the room, with Dani leaving soon after. Still unsure, if he was just being paranoid, he decided to give it one more day to be certain.

Devin decided this would be the last night he would devote to spying on his fiancée. If his suspicions weren't proven, he would put this behind him and marry Dani as planned, without question. He had been sitting in the rental for a couple of hours and was about to leave, when the headlights of a customized, black truck, pull along the curb, two houses behind him. Watching in the rearview mirror, he waited to see who would exit the vehicle. Perplexed, Devin wondered why the occupant hadn't left the truck. Was the driver waiting for someone? After about thirty minutes, the driver finally exited. He had his answer. It was Maalik.

Slumping in his seat, so not to be seen, Devin watched Maalik walk up the street to Dani's house. He watched him ring her doorbell and she let him inside. It was killing him not to know what was going on inside that house.

Over an hour later, Maalik still hadn't come out. Devin was beside himself. What were they doing? A few minutes later, the house went dark. That was his answer.

Devin was so focused on what was going on inside Dani's house, that he never noticed the car that made a U-turn from its parking spot. The sedan had been hidden from Devin's view by Maalik's truck. The driver of the car had come for his own answers. The driver of the sedan was Tor Hudson.

After pondering on what to do next, Devin exited the car and headed up the walkway to Dani's home. He quietly let himself into her house and followed the familiar sounds of ecstasy to her bedroom. The couple was so involved in loving each other, they never knew he was in the house.

Devin stood in the shadows of the darkened doorway, watching another man thrust into his soon-to-be wife. The only illumination in the entire house, was from two dimly lit wall scones above the king-sized bed, enabling him to witness everything.

He observed the expression of pure delight on Dani's face. A look of completion he never saw when they made love. He listened, while another man told her how much he enjoyed being inside of her. Devin listened, while his fiancée told this man, she loved what he was doing to her.

Not able to handle any more humiliation, Devin quietly retraced his steps and made his way outside to his car. He was shaking by the time he had gotten behind the wheel. Struggling to control his emotions, he clenched his fists with rage. How could she do that to him? How could she accept his proposal, his ring, when she was screwing someone else?

Not wanting to leave, Devin waited in his car, until Maalik surfaced. The sun was just peeking over the horizon when saw the front door open and Maalik stepped outside. Maalik's expression was that of a man who was fully sated; a man who had thoroughly fucked his fiancée. With each step Maalik took, walking back to his vehicle, Devin's rage festered to a slow and even burn.

Waiting until Maalik started his truck and drove passed, Devin started his vehicle and followed him from the neighborhood.

☐

Chapter 42

Justin

Justin Graham lay in a bed he swore he would never sleep in again. When he left Anastasia's house, he hadn't planned on coming back, ever. But here he was, back in his old room. The room he moved into a year ago, after realizing he had made a terrible mistake in marrying her.

Carefully, he shifted from lying on his back onto his good side. His mind replayed what transpired, once he reached the house the previous evening. The staff had heard the news of the arrests and were at a loss for what to do next. He wasn't much help; he didn't know the procedure the authorities would take in their case against the Stanton's. Besides, his first priority was his daughter, Cara.

Once he arrived, he spoke with Virginia, Cara's nanny, to get some insight on how to approach his daughter. Virginia had been helpful, by staying with him, while he tried to be a father to her. Because he had little interaction with the little girl, she didn't warm up to him. She only asked for her mother. After a while, Justin gave up, with Virginia promising to help him as much as she could.

One thing was for certain, he would take his daughter back home with him. He had no intentions of bringing her up, as her mother had been raised. The child needed a parent who would love her and be there for her. Justin was determined to be that parent, whatever it took.

He contacted his attorney, to see if there would be any repercussions against his business behind Anastasia and Roland's arrests. He was assured there would be none since Anastasia's money was held in a separate trust, apart from the corporation and her father's money. He would not have to start a new business after all. At least that was one thing he didn't have to worry about.

He also learned Rosemary Stanton, Anastasia's mother, had her own family money and would not be affected financially by her husband's transgressions. It seemed, his soon-to-be ex-wife was not broke after all, thanks to her father who planned for just such a situation.

She would at least have an income once she was released from prison.

Justin planned to be at her sentencing, asking for leniency. He didn't feel she should spend much time in jail, if at all. After everything that happened between them, Anastasia was still Cara's mother. Although she offered to give up her rights to their daughter, he would not accept that. Cara still needed her. Besides, he felt guilty for his part in their mess of a marriage. It was the least that he could do.

Sighing, Justin got up from his bed. He had put off the inevitable long enough. He knew it would be a difficult journey, but he loved Cara and would make sure she knew that; no matter what.

☐

Chapter 43

Jayden

Jayden sat in BJ's Coffee Shop stunned, at what his brother was telling him. He and Hannah had come to the diner to have breakfast when his phone rang. It was Anderson calling, to fill him in on what transpired at the gala.

He and Hannah had planned to attend the gala, but at the last minute decided not to go. They opted to stay in bed, enjoying each other and had only surfaced that morning. They hadn't had the chance to get any news.

After learning of the danger, he was glad they hadn't gone. From what he could gather from Anderson, it was not the place to be after all. He just hoped the incidents, wouldn't halt the foundation's progress.

"Baby, what happened?" Hannah asked after he clicked off. She had been watching his facial expressions the entire time he was on the phone and knew something was wrong.

"Wow," Jayden whispered, as he drew a hand down his face. The news was overwhelming.

"You remember Jean and Evan, right? The party we went to at my brother's?" Hannah nodded. "Well it seems there had been several attempts on Jean's life and it all came to a head at the gala," he told her. Hannah's eyes widened.

Jayden went on to explain the first incident with the snake, followed by the tire that was shot. He continued with Jean's near-death experience with the tainted smoothie and wound it up, with her ex-husband's involvement, and the final attempt at the gala.

"Wow is right," Hannah agreed, shaking her head slowly in amazement. "So this Veda person was the one the whole time trying to kill Jean and not her ex-husband?" Jayden nodded, still stunned at the turn of events.

"And...that wasn't the only attempt at murder that night, he further informed her. Hannah's jaw dropped, as he explained Veda's involvement in Justin Graham's mishaps, and how it wasn't Veda who stabbed him, but his vindictive wife.

"Okay, wait a minute. Anastasia was not the one who hired Veda to kill her husband?" Hannah was beyond bewildered at this point.

"Nope. Anastasia's father, by way of a gangster, who is Veda's cousin I might add, put the hit out on Justin. Anastasia knew nothing of her father's plot. She was there to execute her own revenge." Jayden shook his head at the absurdity of it all.

"And Justin Graham used to date Paige, your sister-in-law?" Hannah asked, trying to keep all the players straight.

"Yep. If it hadn't been for Justin's asinine actions, Anderson and Paige probably wouldn't be married today."

"But at this point, everyone seems to be okay and all those involved in the scheme have been arrested," Jayden concluded.

"Does your family always have this much drama?" Hannah asked with a chuckle.

"Lady, you don't know the half of it," he told her with a half grin.

Chapter 44

KT

KT raised her tousled head and peeked out from underneath the covers, squinting at the sun-filled room. She winced at the sudden pain that shot through her body, brought on by that small movement. Slowly she turned her head to peer at the other side of the king sized bed, only to find it empty. Closing her eyes, she tried not to move. She heard running water coming from the adjoining bathroom.

"Ah, you're awake," Eric noticed when KT opened her eyes again.

"Yes and very sore." She carefully propped herself against the headboard.

Eric leaned over to kiss her. "I figured as much. We were quite active last night," he reminded her with a grin. "But Kaitlin, seriously, you should have warned me from the start. If I'd known it had been that long for you, I would have been gentler." Eric was concerned.

After they wrapped up their cases, Eric picked KT up that evening for dinner. Instead of taking her home afterward, he suggested coming back to his place for drinks, to continue their date. Drinks were forgotten the moment the garage door closed. They had barely made it into the house before they were tearing each other's clothes off. Starting in the kitchen, they worked their way throughout the house, ending in Eric's bedroom.

"Who's complaining," she told him. She certainly wasn't.

KT grinned, when she recalled all the positions and rooms, they had romped through the night before. Once their clothes were discarded in the kitchen, Eric had taken her on and over the kitchen table. From there, they moved to the living room, where she straddled him on an overstuffed chair. After that, they finally made it to his bed, where they spent the remainder of the night, thoroughly enjoying each other.

"Clearly, your body is complaining," he stated with a raised brow. "Now for some relief." Kissing her again, Eric lifted KT from the bed, carrying her to the soothing bath he had prepared.

Chapter 45

Maalik

Maalik walked into Hudson Investigations, to check in for his next assignment. After leaving Dani, in the early hours of the morning, he stopped home to shower and change. He hated sneaking around but thought it was best since she and Devin were officially still together. Although, after last night, he hoped that would change.

They spent the night in each other's arms, after finally moving from the floor to her bedroom. After confessing his feelings, Maalik found she felt the same. But after spotting the huge diamond engagement ring on Dani's finger, he wanted to know what she planned to do about Devin.

Maalik wanted her for himself, but at the same time, wondered if he was doing the right thing, by coming between them. He had only known her for a short period. He asked himself if being with Dani was what he really wanted. Did he truly love her or was this only lust that would cool with time?

He had many questions floating around in his head and he wanted to make sure of the answers before he broke up a couple headed to the altar. Furthermore, he wasn't sure of what Dani wanted. He wondered if she had doubts about Devin, to begin with. It was too easy for her to leave him, without trying to work out their differences. He felt she could have told Devin at any time, the reasons she wouldn't marry him, instead of running away to Toronto.

Putting his thoughts on the back burner for the time being, he walked into Tor's office to catch up on the day's agenda.

#

Tor was troubled. After Maalik dropped him off at home from the airport, he got to thinking about some of the questions he asked about Devin and Dani. At first, he thought the questions were just routine, but the more he thought about it, he felt they weren't.

Acting on a hunch, he drove to Dani's, just in time to see Maalik enter her house. Not knowing what to think of this, and hoping he was wrong, he waited to see what would happen next. However, after a while, it didn't appear Maalik was leaving anytime soon. He was sure of it, once the lights were turned off in the house.

Devin was his friend and he had hired his firm to do a job for him. Tor didn't want this thing with Maalik to come between their friendship. Not only that, Maalik was sent to do a job, not to fall into bed with the client's girlfriend.

On the other hand, Maalik was also a friend. Tor understood how things could happen, with the best self-control. He was at odds, as to what to do about the situation.

Tor thought over his determination to be with his wife Andee. One thing he knew for certain, Devin would never hear from him that one of his employees was sleeping with his fiancée. This was something Dani needed to handle. He tried not to pry into others' relationships. Devin may be a friend, but so was Dani and Maalik.

He looked up when Maalik appeared in his doorway. "Come in Maalik and close the door," Tor instructed him. "Have a seat." Maalik did as he was told. Tor rubbed his chin with a forefinger before he spoke again.

"How long have you been sleeping with Dani?" Tor got right to business. He didn't believe in making small talk when important issues needed to be addressed.

Maalik's eyes widen at Tor's matter-of-fact question. He thought he'd been careful in gleaning information from him. He should have known better. Tor was the best in his field. He should have known he couldn't get anything by him.

"What gave it away?" Maalik asked. There was no need to deny it. He was sure it was written all over his face.

"It's not so much as what you said or did, it was more of a feeling. I became suspicious because you never talked about the clients once a job was done. This was the first time. And I should tell you, I followed you to Dani's last night," he told him.

Maalik sighed. Out of everything that happened, he hated deceiving his best friend. He wondered what Tor would do now.

As if reading his mind, Tor spoke. "Dude, I'm not angry at you or anything. Hell, I would be a hypocrite if I were. That's basically how Andee and I wound up together. Although Jayden had broken things off with her, it wouldn't have mattered. I was determined to go after her just the same. They weren't married. But I just wished you would have confided in me. We're friends," Tor told him.

Maalik breathed a sigh of relief. "I guess I didn't tell you, because I didn't know how you would react."

Maalik swiped a hand down his face. "We first got together in Toronto. She had broken up with Devin and had no plans to get back with him. But when he showed up, well…"

"They patched things up," Tor finished his sentence for him. "My friend, the only thing I am going to tell you is, make sure this is what you want and be careful. I don't think Devin will give her up easily," Tor warned him.

Chapter 46

Dani

Dani walked into the office, all smiles. She had a wonderful night with Maalik. They talked and discovered their shared feelings. She didn't think it was possible, but she felt as if she had won the lottery by being with Maalik.

"Wow, with that smile, I take it Devin's home," Andee commented, when Dani neared her desk.

Dani's smile wavered. She had forgotten about Devin. He was supposed to be home the next day and she didn't have a clue, as to what she was going to do about their relationship. She and Maalik had talked about being together, but he left the final decision up to her. What was she going to do?

"Good morning Andee," she greeted her friend. Not knowing what to say on the subject of Devin, she skirted the comment.

Andee was just about to push further when Paige waddled into the reception area.

"Paige, what are you doing here?" Dani asked her. Paige was due any day and should have been home resting, and not hanging around the office.

Paige rolled her eyes. "Don't you start too. I already got a tongue-lashing from Andee, not to mention my husband, for wanting to come in. I made a deal with Anderson. He would drive me to and from work. So stop your worrying," she told her friends.

"Besides, I haven't seen either one of you since that mess at the gala with Evan, Jean, and Justin. I got the full scoop on Jean's case from my brother, but only bits and pieces about Justin's. I was hoping Andee would have the details from her husband," Paige commented with a raised brow at Andee.

"Well you know how Tor is about his business," Andee stated with a shrug. "But yes, I know the full story, so gather around girls," she added with a satisfied grin.

Andee told her friends the details that were involved in Justin's murder attempts. From the stripper who was commissioned to do the job, to Anastasia's attempt of her own at the gala.

"So, Anastasia *and* her father were out to get Justin?" Paige asked. Andee nodded. Dani only listened without comment. She had already heard the story from Maalik.

"Dani, you were at the gala, did you see any of this?" Paige asked.

"No, I didn't stay long. I guess all of the mayhem had gotten underway after I left. It wasn't any fun without you ladies being there. And you know how I hate going places alone."

"That's right, Devin was out of town. Is he back?"

"No. I expect him to be back sometime tomorrow." Out of the corner of her eye, Dani could see the questioning expression on Andee's face. The office phone rang, saving her from more scrutiny. While Andee handled the call, Dani took this opportunity to escape.

"Paige, since you're here, can I get your opinion on something?" Dani asked her.

"Sure, your office or mine?"

"Mine, what I have to show you is in my office," she told her. Dani breathed a sigh of relief. Andee was too caught up in a conversation with her mother, to be concerned about her.

Dani didn't have to show Paige anything. She just needed to talk to her without Andee. She loved Andee, but she was married to Maalik's boss and couples do tend to tell each other mostly everything. She chose her office because it was farthest away from the reception area *and* Andee. She couldn't take a chance she might overhear their conversation.

Once they reached her office, Dani closed the door while Paige lowered her baby bulk into a chair.

"What was it you wanted my opinion on," Paige asked her.

Dani took her seat and paused before she spoke. How was she going to break this news?

"Paige, I think I'm in love," she blurted.

"Well of course you're in love. You and Devin are finally engaged to be married. And how are the plans coming along anyway? I know Devin said he didn't want to wait." Paige was a little confused. Why was Dani making this widely-known declaration?

Dani shook her head. "Paige, I'm in love with someone else," she told her.

Paige's eyes widened. "What do you mean you're in love with someone else?" She was shocked at this revelation. The only man she knew in Dani's life was Devin.

After she'd gotten back from Toronto, Dani finally shared with her friends, why she ended things with Devin. However, she left out the part about meeting Maalik on the train, and what transpired afterwards. All Paige and Andee knew was she and Devin had come home engaged.

Without hesitation, Dani revealed what she had been holding back; right up to being with Maalik the night before.

Paige was stunned. "Dani…I don't know what to say. What about Devin? What are you going to do? Do you want to be with Maalik?" All Paige could do was ask questions.

"That's just the thing. I don't know what I'm going to do. I love Devin, but it's not the way he loves me. And with Maalik, it's different. It's like we get each other. You know? Devin is sweet and gentle, whereas Maalik manhandles me. He doesn't treat me like I'm a delicate piece of crystal that might break if he touches me the wrong way. Maalik makes me laugh. He brings excitement to my life. He takes control and doesn't ask me my opinion about every little thing like Devin does. Paige, Maalik gets me."

"Wow!" Paige just stared at her best friend. "I have never heard you speak this way, especially about Devin. I thought you two were happy."

"I thought I was happy too, until I met Maalik. It's like he flipped a switch inside of me. You know?"

"Does Devin suspect anything?" Paige asked. "You did say when he found you in Toronto, you were with Maalik." Dani shook her head.

"Devin never really questioned me about Maalik, because he knew he was there at Tor's request," she told her.

"Honey…all I can tell you to do is to follow your heart. And if it says to be with Maalik, then that's it. But you need to put things right with Devin. Dani that man loves you."

"I know. I have some thinking to do before he gets home tomorrow. And Paige, I would appreciate you not saying anything to Andee. Tor is Maalik's boss and he doesn't know anything about this. I don't want to put him in the middle. He's friends with both Maalik and Devin."

Paige nodded her agreement, just as the first contraction hit her. "Oh!" she exclaimed, as she bent forward.

"Paige, what's the matter?" Dani stood, concerned.

"Call Anderson…I think I'm in labor."

Dani grabbed the phone, as she yelled for Andee. The baby was coming.

Chapter 47

Dani

"Hey baby, where are you? I'm home and I can't wait to see you." Devin called Dani on her cell, after not getting an answer, at the office or her home. He had been thinking about their situation all day, and finally, he had the answer.

"Devin, hi…I'm at the hospital with the gang. Paige had a baby boy," she told him. Dani had to put her finger in her ear, to be able to hear him. Everyone was in Paige's room, admiring the baby.

She and Andee made Paige as comfortable as they could, while they waited for Anderson to arrive. By the time he had gotten there, Page's contractions were about ten minutes apart, giving them plenty of time, considering the hospital was only five minutes away. Anderson wanted them to call an ambulance for her, and meet them at the hospital, but Paige wouldn't hear of it. She wanted him there with her from start to finish.

By the time they made it to the hospital, her water had broken and the contractions were down to two minutes apart. While Anderson and Paige were in delivery, she and Andee had called the family and friends, who were now all in Paige's room.

Stepping out into the corridor to hear better, Dani continued her conversation.

"I see you made it back early. How was your trip?" She wasn't interested in his trip, but she didn't know what else to say.

"It was...enlightening," he told her with a frown. "I really would like to see you. Do you think you could leave and come to my house? I've cooked us dinner and I just want to spend some time with my fiancée," he told her with feigned joy.

"Sure, I'm on my way," she told him before clicking off her phone.

Dani sighed. This was as good a time as any, to break things off with him. She decided she needed to leave her relationship with Devin, whether she was with Maalik or not. Although she loved him, she realized she wasn't really in love with him. He deserved better than a half-baked relationship.

"Hey Dani, how is Paige and the baby?" This was Taylor asking. She and Dain had just arrived.

Dani hugged her soon-to-be sister-in-law. "Hi, Taylor. Hey little brother," she spoke to Dain, kissing his cheek.

"Mother and son are doing great. And Anderson is right by their side with his chest stuck out, I might add." She chuckled. Anderson had not left Paige's side for one second.

"Hey, could you two tell Paige and Anderson I had to leave?" She asked them.

"Where are you headed off to?" Dain asked.

"Devin has been out of town and he's back and anxious to see me," she told him, with a manufactured smile.

"Taylor, can I have a minute with my sister?"

"Sure, I am anxious to see the baby. Dani, I will see you later, and tell Devin hello for me." Taylor hugged Dani again, before entering the room to join the rest of the crowd.

"What's wrong?" Dain asked his sister, as soon as the door closed. He knew her; knew her well. Something wasn't right, and he wanted to know what was going on.

"Dain, can this wait? I will fill you in on everything later, okay?"

Dani didn't want to get into it with her brother. If he knew she was about to break things off with Devin, for good this time, and why, he would insist on coming with her. This was going to be difficult enough without him instigating.

"Only if you promise to fill me in with what's going on with you."

Dani nodded. She hugged her brother and left.

Dain watched his sister until she got on the elevator, and then he too joined the host of family and friends who came to see the new baby.

#

"Hey Dain, how are things?" Tor asked, making room for him in the crowded room.

"I hope everything is okay," he said more to himself than he did to Tor. He was beginning to have an uneasy feeling about whatever was bothering Dani.

"What's up?" Tor asked, not liking the sound of Dain's answer.

"I don't know. My sister just left here on her way to see Devin, but she didn't look too happy about it. Do you know what's going on?" Tor only shook his head with a slight shrug.

"I'm sure she's probably just overwhelmed. Did she tell you she was with Paige when she went into labor?" Tor redirected. Although he appeared nonchalant about the situation, he was feeling anything but.

"Hey, excuse me a moment. I need to check in with my office," he told Dain.

Knowing the situation between Dani and Maalik, Tor wondered about her unhappiness with seeing Devin.

He worried she may be about to break things off with him. Though Tor didn't believe Devin was violent, he also didn't think it would hurt to play it safe just in case.

He stepped out into the corridor to call Maalik. After trying his line a couple of times and not getting an answer, he called KT.

#

KT clicked off her phone. Tor had given her an address to check on. He also gave her a quick rundown, of what was going on, and wanted her to be on the premises just as a precaution.

"Eric…" She started regretfully.

Eric sighed. "Don't tell me, you gotta go?" he finished for her. They were at his place having dinner. Wiping her mouth with her napkin, KT nodded.

"Do you need me to tag along," he asked hopefully.

Eric knew KT was good at her job, and had been doing it long before he met her, but since they had become close, he worried about her. He knew her occupation was just as dangerous as his.

"Nope," she told him rising from her chair to kiss him. "But you can save dessert for me. This shouldn't take long," she told him.

Eric walked her outside to her bike. He kissed her again before she donned her helmet and watched, as she rode out of sight.

Chapter 48

Devin

Dani stepped over the threshold after Devin opened the door for her. She was not happy with what she was about to do. She let Devin kiss her after he closed the door behind her. Dani followed him into the formal dining room she designed for him.

When she entered the room, she noticed that Devin had set a formal table with three place settings. Perplexed, she turned to ask him about the third setting.

"Are you expecting someone else to join us for dinner?

"Yes, my guest will be here for dessert," he informed her. "Here, why don't you sit down while I serve you. I'll be right back." He seated her and left the room.

While Devin disappeared into the kitchen, Dani went over in her head what she would say to him. She hated to hurt him, but she would be hurting him more if she dragged this out. She wasn't in love with him and nothing was going to change that.

Devin made several trips to and from the kitchen. He had cooked an excellent meal. He had prepared a crab salad for starters. For the main course, filet mignon with sautéed, crisp mixed vegetables, along with his special four cheeses, and baked potatoes that Dani loved.

Devin surveyed the table, after bringing in the last dish; all of Dani's favorites. At least, she used to love them, he thought, as he poured them each a glass of vintage wine.

"Was your trip successful?" Dani asked, chewing a bit of steak that she wasn't tasting. A knot had formed in her stomach. She dreaded what she was about to do.

"Very successful. I've learned a lot in these past few days. It has been quite an eye-opener." Devin studied her, while he cut into his steak.

Suddenly, Dani didn't feel they were still discussing his trip. It was something in his tone of voice. Was that a sneer she saw? It had come and gone so quickly that she wasn't sure.

"Devin, is there something wrong?" Dani cautiously asked. She could feel there was a storm brewing just beneath the surface. *Could he know?*

"I don't know Dani, is there?" Devin asked her with a deadly calm. He placed his knife and fork on his plate.

Fear began to fill Dani with an instant coldness. So much so, that she began to shiver.

"I mean, you haven't been yourself lately. You haven't been sleeping since…oh, well, since we got back from Toronto," he told her, before taking a sip from his wine glass.

Devin reveled in her unease. *Good. This bitch should be nervous.*

Placing the glass back on the table, Devin continued. "Dani, you're not eating. Aren't you hungry? I planned all of your favorites tonight, right down to dessert," he informed her with a malevolent grin. "Aren't you going to ask me what's for dessert?" Devin taunted her. He wanted to see fear in her eyes.

"Wha…what are we having for dessert?" she asked, clearly upset with the evening's turn of events.

"I'm glad you asked," Devin smirked, before taking another sip from his glass. "We're having your lover, Maalik Wyatt, as the guest of honor for dessert."

Devin took this opportunity to push his mobile phone towards her with one hand, while he produced a handgun with the other.

"Call him!" He ordered, with a pound of his fist; rattling the dishes on the table.

#

Maalik had gotten out of the shower, just as his cell phone rang. He viewed the number displayed but didn't recognize it. Shrugging, he answered anyway.

"Hello?"

#

KT sat outside of the well-manicured estate, tapping her fingers on the steering wheel. She stopped by her place just long enough to park her bike, and hop into her gray Mustang. She mostly used the car when she was conducting surveillance. Sitting on a motorcycle would only draw unwanted attention.

She had been there for about forty-five minutes when a familiar black truck made its way up the street. As it passed, she saw it was Maalik.

"Oh no, oh no, no, no, this cannot be good," she mumbled to herself.

She watched Maalik pull into the driveway and exit the vehicle. When he was let inside the house, she quickly left her car and hustled across the street toward the house, with her weapon tucked in her waistband.

#

Dani let Maalik into the house while trying not to appear frightened. Devin had his gun trained on her from a room just off of the foyer.

"Hey, what's up? What are you doing here?" He asked her. Before she could answer him, Devin hit Maalik from behind, knocking him out cold.

Meanwhile, KT was making her way around to the side of the house, peering into windows, trying to catch a glimpse of what was taking place inside. Not able to see what was going on, from the side windows, she made her way to the back of the house.

Tor had given her a quick assessment of what he thought may happen at Devin Powers' home. He expected Dani to call things off with him and just wanted her there if needed. Although he told her Maalik was involved, he never mentioned that he may show up. For KT, Maalik's presence only spelled trouble.

Devin took an arm and dragged Maalik into the dining room, with Dani preceding him; his handgun pointed at her back. Leaving an unconscious Maalik on the floor, he motioned for her to take her seat.

Terrified, Dani did as she was told. She glanced at Maalik, hoping he was okay. Devin hit him pretty hard.

"Now that your lover is here, why don't you tell me about those sleepless nights you were having? Were you thinking of him? Was the need to be with him keeping you awake in my bed?" Dani stared at him, not knowing what to say.

"ANSWER ME!" He yelled.

"Ye…yes," she managed to stammer out. Dani was scared. She had never seen Devin this way. She never knew he was even capable of such violence.

"Finally the truth!" Devin rolled his eyes and gestured with his weaponless hand, in exasperation.

"Wanna know how I know about him?" He asked, but not expecting an answer. "While I was inside you, you called out his name! Not my name…but HIS!" Devin waved the gun at Maalik. Dani closed her eyes and moaned.

His expression darkened. "That was the first clue. And I'm sure you can guess by now, that I wasn't out of town. Last night, when you let him into your house, I was there watching. I waited for him to come out; hoping, praying that I was wrong about you. But low and behold, I knew better, once you turned out the lights." Dani felt as if she would faint.

"You see Dani," Devin continued, moving closer to her. "I let myself into your house last night, while you were in bed with him. I saw you fucking him. I heard what you said to him. How good it was. How you loved the way he made you feel," Devin sneered.

He used the shaft of the gun to caress her face. "Why did you have to go and mess everything up for us, huh? We were happy until you ran off to Toronto. We could have worked through our issues, if you would have just given us a chance."

Dani could only look at him with wide-eyed fear. She couldn't respond to his rantings.

"Well, you know what? I've decided, if I can't be happy, you sure as hell aren't going to be. Devin leveled the gun at her.

I'm going to die, I'm going to die, she chanted inwardly. She closed her eyes to what was sure to come—death.

A shot rang out and Dani fell to the floor.

☐

Chapter 49

The Aftermath

"Dani… Dani baby wake up." This was Maalik. He was trying to get her to open her eyes.

Dani came to with a start. After the gunshot, she passed out, falling to the floor. Remembering what happened, she quickly sat up, to find the house swarming with people, mostly the police.

"What happened?" She asked Maalik, as he helped her to her feet. But before he could explain, Dani spotted Devin's motionless body lying on the floor.

"Maalik…what?…Oh my God…"

Devin was dead. Dani sobbed uncontrollably, while Maalik held her. Everything she experienced that evening came rushing back.

#

"Looks like I should have accompanied you after all," Eric told KT. She called him immediately after Devin was shot.

Shaking her head, KT closed her eyes. "This was supposed to be a routine job. I was here for precautionary reasons only," she told him.

"Well, it was good you were here. From the note he left, he had planned to do a whole lot more damage had you not stopped him, "Eric told her.

KT had made her way to the back of the house where she found an unlocked door. She followed the voices to the dining room. What she found was Maalik lying on the floor unconscious and Devin Powers waving a gun at Dani. She didn't have a chance to make her presence known, before he leveled his gun at Dani, to pull the trigger. Without further thought, KT shot Devin in the chest, killing him instantly.

"What do you mean," she asked Eric.

"It seems your boy there," he stated, pointing to Devin with his chin, "had planned for this to be a murder-suicide. He stated in his note, if he couldn't be with Ms. Sinclair, no one would. He planned to kill her, Maalik, and then himself. Tor had good instincts on this one."

"Dani, Dani…" Dain had arrived with Tor, who informed him of his sister's involvement after KT phoned him.

Dani pulled from Maalik's embrace, to hug her brother.

"Are you ok?" he asked. He held her away from him to look her over for wounds. Seeing none he embraced her again.

"I'm fine," she sniffed, still shaken by what happened.

"If that asshole wasn't dead I'd…" Dain was furious. Had he thought for a second that his sister was in any danger, he would not have let her leave the hospital, let alone come to this house of horrors.

"Dani, what happened? He was still unclear about most of the details. All Tor would tell him was Devin was dead, and Dani needed him.

Holding her brother tighter, Dani looked over at Maalik before she spoke.

"Devin found out about me and Maalik," she said just above a whisper.

Dain noticed the man standing near them for the first time, since entering the room. He eyed him carefully, as he held onto his sister.

"When you say found out, what does that mean?" He asked, not liking where this was headed.

Pulling from his embrace, Dani continued. "Dain, this is Maalik Wyatt, Maalik my brother." She made the introductions before she delved deeper into the tangled mess. They each nodded at the other.

"I met Maalik on the train to Toronto. He was sent by Tor to protect me at Devin's request. Maalik and I became close, and…" she trailed off when she spotted the coroner wheeling Devin's body from the room.

Swallowing, she pulled her eyes from the scene. "We became close while I was away. I had come here to tell Devin it was over when he pulled… pulled a gun on me." She closed her eyes and cleared her throat, before continuing.

"He ranted and raved about how he watched Maalik and I last night." Dani noticed Maalik's brows rise, at this revelation.

"He forced me to call Maalik to come here. Once he got inside, Devin hit him over the head and dragged him in here…where he…where he…"

"He would have killed her if KT hadn't been here…" Maalik finished for her. Dani had buried herself back into Dain's embrace.

"Who's KT?" Dain asked. He would be forever grateful to the guy for saving his sister.

"She's over there talking to Detective Valero," Maalik informed him.

Dain took a double take at the woman Maalik referred to as KT. He fully expected a man and not this gorgeous female.

"Who is she?" He asked. Dain gave the woman his full attention, as his eyes perused her body. Catching himself, he brought his mind and eyes back to his sister.

"Kaitlin Ellis works for Tor," Maalik told him.

Dain watched the body language between the woman and the detective. He could tell they were together. As he watched KT, his actions began to disturb him, but he couldn't help himself. Dain was slipping back into his old ways. This was not good, considering he was to be married in a few weeks.

"And she was the one..." Dain asked, still scoping out the private detective.

"The one who shot Devin, yes," Maalik observed Dain's lustful interest in KT. He remembered Dani telling him her brother was engaged to be married.

Deciding Dain's behavior was none of his business, Maalik went on to explain how KT happened to be there. He hadn't known himself until after he woke from being knocked unconscious by Devon. He had no clue as to what happened between the time he arrived and waking up on the floor. KT filled him in on the parts he missed. He relayed to Dain as much as he could, considering he was out cold for most of it.

"Maalik, I'm so sorry I called you to come here. I didn't know what else to do," Dani told him, wiping tears from her eyes. She was trying to pull herself together.

Devin had forced her to lure him there, without warning him or he would have killed her on the spot. She had no other choice.

"Shhh, baby. It's not your fault," he told her after she shifted from her brother's arms to his.

While Maalik comforted his sister, Dain saw his opportunity to thank KT personally, when the detective left the room.

"I hear I owe you for Dani's life," Dain told KT when he joined her.

"And you are?" She asked. She knew that look; this man was on the prowl. KT frowned.

"I'm Dain Sinclair, Dani's brother, Ms. Ellis.

"Well Mr. Sinclair, I only did what I was trained and hired to do," she informed him, frowning deeper. "Excuse me," she told him, before leaving him to join Maalik and Dani.

Dain studied her shapely backside as she walked across the room. He rationalized his behavior, by telling himself it didn't hurt to look. Besides, he wasn't married—yet.

Dain shifted his gaze to his sister. He felt guilty. He should have at least come with her. He knew something wasn't right and should have acted on his instincts. He sighed. He figured, no one really knew anyone. Never in his wildest nightmares would he have thought Devin Powers would have tried to harm his sister.

"Maalik, you should get that cut on the back of your head checked," KT told him.

After she made the call to Detective Valero, she called for an ambulance, when she couldn't get Maalik to come around immediately. KT knew Dani had merely passed out and would be fine, so she was more concerned with the gash on Maalik's head. But by the time the police and paramedics had arrived, she had finally gotten him to sit up.

"I'm fine," he said, before wincing from the touch of his fingers.

"You are not fine," KT told him. "And Miss Sinclair, why don't you go with him and get yourself checked out too?

Dani nodded, pulling Maalik in the direction of the waiting paramedics.

Eric nodded at Maalik and Dani, as they passed him. "What did that guy want?" Eric asked, referring to Dain, who was still eyeing KT. She glanced in Dain's direction, while Eric observed him with suspicion.

"He's Dani's brother. He just wanted to thank me for saving his sister," she told him; dismissing Dain's obvious attention.

"And from the looks of him, I know just how he wants to thank you too." Eric frowned. "The nerve of that guy. He should be more concerned about his sister than trying to figure out how to get into your pants," he told an amused KT.

"Are you jealous?" She asked him with a smile.

"No, I'm just saying…ok maybe a little bit," he confessed after KT folded her arms at his obvious lie.

"Well, Detective Eric Valero, you don't have to worry about Mr. Sinclair. I am all yours," she told a grinning Eric.

"For that my lady, you get extra dessert when we get home," he promised with a wink.

☐

Chapter 50

Justin

Justin Graham stood in the doorway of his daughter's bedroom, watching her sleep. He had packed up Cara and her nanny, Virginia, and moved them into his home. It had been a rough few days with Cara crying for her mother. It was a good thing he had the foresight to ask Virginia to come along with them. She was the only stable presence in the child's life at the moment.

Virginia had been hesitant at first. She hadn't lived anywhere except Raleigh. He knew she would have to leave her family and friends if she took the position, but he needed her. Cara needed her. He promised, that if she couldn't adapt after three months, he would pay her expenses back to North Carolina.

"Mr. Graham, may I speak with you for a moment?" Virginia asked Justin. He had made his way back to the common room where Virginia was folding clothes.

Justin's heart sank. Even though it hadn't been anywhere near three months, he thought he knew what she wanted. She wanted to go home. He thought she had settled in nicely and liked it there. He was beginning to relax, especially after Cara started warming up to him, due to Virginia's help.

Justin sighed, "Yes Virginia, what is it?"

She rose from the couch to address him. "Well, I wanted to talk to you about your clothes or should I say a lack of them," Virginia informed him.

Noticing that he was puzzled, she continued. "I noticed you like to roam around the house at night, with nothing on, and…I don't think it's appropriate with Cara being in the house sir," she informed him.

Virginia had innocently gotten up in the middle of the night to check on Cara when she heard him in the kitchen. After she checked on the child, she started into the kitchen, before she was stopped short by his nude body. Justin was in the midst of his nightly refrigerator raid in the buff. Virginia was startled at first, but she couldn't get herself to leave. She watched him move about the room, gathering various items for his sandwich. Unlike KT's view, Virginia was treated to all of Justin.

After getting an eye-opening view of her employer, she made it back to her room, completely aroused. Virginia had always found Justin attractive, but never let on, because of her employment and because he was married. When they both lived in Anastasia's house, she had caught him looking at her a few times, but that was all. She never made anything of it. But now, she was in his home and he was in the process of divorce, she hoped he would look at her, as more than just Cara's nanny.

Justin was embarrassed. It hadn't dawned on him that he should stop his routine of walking around nude, after his shower. He had lived in his house too long, alone. Virginia was right. There were some things he needed to change, now that she and Cara were living there. Even in his embarrassment, he noticed she said he should consider Cara and not herself.

Justin had always liked Virginia. He noticed how attractive she was from the start. Obviously, his wife had noticed too. While she was living in her house, Anastasia had the young woman dress, as if she were an old maid.

He noticed the moment Virginia moved into his home, her manner of dress had changed. He admired the figure-hugging jeans and the low-cut tops that showed off her ample assets, something he hadn't noticed before, because of the dowdy clothes she had always worn.

"Virginia, you're right. I will make sure I am fully clothed from now on. I apologize if I offended you," he added. "And please, if I am to address you by your first name, by all means, call me Justin." He had been meaning to tell her to drop the Mr. Graham when she first moved in.

Virginia smiled. "Thank you. And Justin," she added. "You didn't offend me," she told him with her smile widening. "Good night." With that, Virginia turned to make her way to her room.

Justin watched her with a smile of his own.

Epilogue

Dani watched her brother and his new bride dance at their reception. She grinned when she recalled the look of panic that had taken over Dain's face when it was his turn to recite his vows. Dani thought he would keel over before he could finish them. But after the initial scare, he had gotten through the ceremony just fine.

"I see Dain has gotten over his stage fright, Paige commented. She held baby Reed in her arms. It had been seven weeks since she had the baby and she was still in awe of her little miracle.

"Yes. I can't believe my brother is finally married. I never thought I would see this day."

"Yeah, most of us thought he would be a skirt hound forever," Andee commented, as she and Tor joined them.

"Dani, how are you doing?" Tor asked. He felt responsible for what had taken place at Devin's. However, never in a million years would he have thought Devin was capable of killing her or anyone else for that matter.

"Tor, I'm fine. Stop worrying. As I told you before, there was no way you could have known Devin would crack like that. None of us could," she reassured him. "I thank you for having the foresight to send KT, or things would have been a helluva lot different."

Tor glanced towards KT. She was laughing at something Eric had said to her. Before Eric Valero, he had never seen her smile, let alone laugh. He smiled. Eric was good for Kaitlin. Tor then switched his gaze from them to the happy couple.

Taylor had left the dance floor to visit with some of the guests. Tor watched Dain's gaze repeatedly zero in on KT. He noticed his interest in her at Devin's. Tor shook his head at his friend. If he didn't get it together, his marriage was most certainly doomed.

Sighing at Dain's antics, he shifted his attention to Jayden and Hannah. They seemed to be truly happy together. Jayden never took his eyes off of her. Tor wondered if it was partially due to Dain's still-roving eye. He observed Jayden more than once eyeing Dain when he tried to discreetly inspect every single female in the room.

"So Kylon, you now have a new brother," Anderson commented on Taylor's marriage to Dain.

"Yeah, well, I was still a little skeptical. I wondered if he would go through with the marriage. Men like Dain Sinclair don't change overnight. Some of the guys had a pool going to see how long it would take before he ran out of the church screaming." Kylon and Anderson chuckled.

"Where is my sister? Anderson asked Kylon. Kylon and Mia were a couple.

"She went off with your wife to help with the baby.

In a couple of days, he planned to take Mia away to propose. He watched how her face lit up when she held her nephew. He wanted to witness that same look when she held their child.

"Is Dani ok?" Kylon asked Anderson. She and Maalik had joined the crowd on the dance floor. He noticed during the ceremony that she appeared uneasy. He guessed, with all she'd been through, it would take some time to recover.

"Yeah, she seems to be, but you never know. I'm glad she has Maalik to help her through this. I'm sure it helps that he can relate, considering he experienced the nightmare with her." Kylon nodded.

#

Dain took another peek at the lovely Kaitlin Tamara Ellis. He sighed. He was now a married man and he knew he should be acting accordingly. He took a long look around the room at the happy couples in attendance.

He spotted Evan and Jean, who had gone through hell to be together; Anderson and Paige, Tor and Andee. But what interested him the most was Jayden and Hannah. He still couldn't get over the fact they were a couple.

Dain lingered on Hannah. He had loved her when they were together, although she and no one else would ever know. She was by far, out of all his women, besides his wife, a real woman of substance. He had found himself falling for her and it scared him. So much so, he dumped her and moved on to the next woman. Out of everything he'd done in his life, Hannah Pierce was his one regret. She had deserved his love. But at the time, he hadn't been man enough to give it to her. He genuinely wished her well.

Dain hoped Hannah found the man who would give her more than words.